CW00404813

Ian Carroll is an award-winning author, with all I Kindle.

Ian is the author of the 'A-Z of Bloody Horror'

Water May Contain Mermaids', 'Antique Shop',

of the horror books *'My Name is Ishmael', 'Demon Pirates Vs Vikings – Blackhorn's Revenge', 'The Lover's Guide to Internet Dating' and 'Valentine's Day'*. Some of these books are also in the collection **'Late Night Tales'** – available in hardback, paperback and on Kindle

'Hammer Horror' is also the first book in **'The Movie Fans Have Their Say'** series of Books, with many more planned for the future.

He is also the author of the music books –

'Lemmy: Memories of a Rock 'N' Roll Legend' – which was a #1 in the UK, USA, Canada, France, and Germany – *'Ronnie James Dio: Man on the Silver Mountain – Memories of a Rock 'N' Roll Icon', 'Leonard Cohen: Just One More Hallelujah', 'Music, Mud and Mayhem: The Official History of the Reading Festival' and 'From Donington to Download: The History of Rock at Donington Park'.*

The First fourteen Volumes of the *'Fans Have Their Say...'* series are also available which include: **KISS, AC/DC, Black Sabbath, Guns 'N Roses, Metallica, Def Leppard, Bon Jovi, Joan Jett, Motley Crue** and **Queen**.

Ian has also written the history section for the Official Reading Festival music site in the UK and has attended the festival 34 times since 1983.

Ian lives with his wife Raine, two sons – Nathan and Stanley a Jack Russell plus the memories of a jet-black witch's cat, called Rex - in Devon, UK.

Facebook.com/iancarrollauthor (Various Book Pages as well)

Message me any thoughts on this or any of my other books at -
iancarrollauthor@me.com

© Ian Carroll 2023

ISBN- 9798713873615

Get

Moist

© Ian Carroll 2023

For my Brother-In-Law

Steven

You are truly My inspiration,

the wind beneath my wings...

Prologue: 'Gudbuy T'Jane'

Sometime in the 1970's

'The Generation Game'

'The Generation Game' was a staple of Saturday evening TV viewing in the UK throughout the glorious 1970's. Presented by the legendary Bruce Forsyth and his host Anthea Redfern – who he later wed, after a brief affair – the show regularly received top ratings in the viewing stakes and around 21 million viewers, especially due to their only being three TV channels to choose from at the time. The show was always a major feature of the 1970's Christmas Television schedule on the BBC, with a special shown in the evening on Christmas Day every year.

The show featured family couples competing against each other for points to get to the final and win a heap of prizes after games such as origami, pottery, dancing, and an end of show acting piece, not dissimilar to the UK's panto season.

A highlight of the show was a 'memory game' where a member of the winning family team would sit in front of a conveyor belt for 45 seconds, as fondue sets, scales, clocks, cutlery sets and more went past, which they then had to remember in order to win them. Who could forget the cheers and screams that would erupt from the hyper studio audience as the 'cuddly toy' went by in front of the finalist's greedy eyes on the fast-moving belt.

The show was also littered with catchphrases which would be repeated in the playground, the workplace and everywhere all over the UK, from 'Nice to see you, to see you nice' to 'good game, good game' to 'Didn't he do well' and 'Give us a twirl'.

In 1978 Bruce was replaced by Larry Grayson, who was also an incredibly popular presenter and with him came his hostess Isla St Clair and a slew of new catchphrases which were right out of the 'Carry On' branch including – 'What a gay day', 'Seems like a nice boy' and the unforgettable 'Shut that door'.

*****

The light and constant tinkling sound of the clinking glasses reverberated around the terrace, bouncing off the walls and filling the tranquil evening, gradually building to a crescendo of alcohol fuelled noise, as the night progressed.

A cocktail party was already in full swing, and the swingiest, grooviest, and most hip chicks and cool guys around were in attendance, mooching in groups, listening to the band who were playing inside the stately home, whilst they all quaffed down copious amounts of expensive European beers, free cocktails, and costly spirits.

It was a cool February evening, but heating lamps were standing on the veranda, to keep all guests warm and all the coolest guys and gals from the outer suburbs to the dead centre of London, had been invited to hang out at the party of the summer, held in Whitchitley Hall, in Sussex, one of the many properties owned by the affluent, charming - yet extremely manipulative - Sébastien Kang.

Kang Jr. was the only son of the multi-millionaire Chinese property tycoon, Kit Kang, who resided on his own in a luxurious palace on Lamma Island, China - running his considerable business empire through nearby Hong Kong; the palace had been built to Kang Snr's specific drawings and requests, featuring over twenty-five bedrooms, eighteen bathrooms, a ballroom and a full-sized theatre that could comfortably seat four hundred guests.

Whitchitley Hall was a similar sized property and had been designed and built to a very close and comparable plan to the palace in China. It was created by Kang Snr., for Kang Jr. as a gift, when he'd shown an interest in moving permanently to the UK to both improve on his already excellent grasp of English and continue and complete his education at Oxford; that was four years ago, and he had now finished his degree course and was globally recognised as an '*International Playboy about town*'.

The sweeping staircase - that majestically led from the first-floor level down to the main entrance - and the hall was filled on virtually every other marble step with people chatting and laughing, with women tossing their hair around to emphasise the points that they had just randomly blurted out to their friends and colleagues.

Then there was a loud '*crash*' from the base of the stairs, as one of the waiting staff bashed a large gong with a huge leather headed mallet, the handle made from an ornate piece of ancient carved ivory. The sound echoed around the hallway and the stairs, as all the partygoers looked up from their conversations in stunned silence, the music finished, and a deathly hush filled the country house and then there

he was.

All eyes focused on the first floor as their host stood at the top of the stairs.

Dressed all in black, Sébastien Kang looked amazing and inspiring - from his black suit by Hugo Boss, to his black Armani shirt and black leather Chelsea boots, he was a formidable host and every part the successful businessman; the immaculate clothing also took the focus a little away from his face.

A black floppy fringe of raven wing coloured hair, hung loosely across his forehead, drooping slightly over his left eye, which was scarred and glazed over white, the '*unseeing eye*' as he referred to it.

Kang had been attacked by an eagle, when visiting Dubai with his father, ten years previously when he was only seventeen, on a 'funding visit to see some sheiks who had an interest in investing in property in China. He had lost sight in his eye when the bird had 'gone wild' when a car had backfired on a trip into the desert, startling the bird which had flown at the nearest thing to him, which happened to be Kang Jnr.

The servant driving the car had been immediately executed, but the bird was spared, as it was one of the Sheikh's prize creatures and thus too expensive to destroy - servants could be replaced they were '*ten a penny*', exquisite and rare eagles couldn't be.

"Welcome to my party, my beautiful people," began Kang as he swept his arm across the whole area, as he commenced his descent of the staircase, people nodding to him and shaking his hand as he glided down the stairs to the hallway. The way that Kang moved was a miracle in itself as he suffered from CMT - Charcot Marie Tooth disease - which was an inherited disorder of his peripheral nervous system. Kang used a cane - which was also jet black, matching his clothes - with a silver jewel encrusted eagles head on top, as an ironic reminder to where his disfigurement had been acquired from. He already had 'hammer toes' where there were curled under all the time, but the extra padding in his boots, made walking not so much of a problem - for the moment - perhaps in twenty or thirty years it might be a different situation altogether. He was aware of the future possibilities of progressive muscle loss but hoped that his vast fortune would be able to help alleviate any problems that might arise – near limitless money worked wonders.

Kang slowly continued down the stairs, still shaking the male guest's hands, kissing the female guest's hands, and smiling back at his guests, as they acknowledged their party host, all at the same time avoiding directly staring at his 'white eye' and the deep healed claw gouges cutting through his eyebrow and across his eyelids to the top of his cheek.

"Please to meet you," he responded to the guests as they all moved to desperately shake the hand of one of the richest men in the

'Western Hemisphere'. Kang commanded respect from the male guests and adoration from all the ladies in attendance, all the females hoping for the possibility of romantic entanglement being on the cards and a life of untold wealth, parties and no more working.

As Kang stepped off the final step of the staircase and onto the polished marble floor, the crowd opened like a parting of the waves and allowed him a clear path towards the ballroom. As he walked briskly through the crowd, someone passed word on to the band and they started up again, playing an extremely funky cover of 'Living for City' by Stevie Wonder. Being 1973, the single was out and had proved a popular follow up to 'Higher Ground' - it had already hit the Top 20 in the UK, and it had been a 'Top Ten Smash' in the States, so everyone knew it and immediately got back to dancing.

The band consisted of three black and three white musicians, with three oriental female backing singers - who immediately caught Kang's eye as he strutted across the dance floor in the direction of the band.

Standing at the front of the stage, in the centre, Kang tapped his cane in rhythm to the music. As the song finally came to an end - that would've made Mr. Wonder extremely proud - the crowd of party guests in the ballroom all applauded and none more so than Kang himself. Placing his cane carefully on the floor, he raised his arms high in the air, clapping his hands and 'whooping', showing his appreciation for '*Rocket 69*' - the band that he'd hired specifically for this evening's entertainment.

They had only been playing together for a short period of time since 1970, two years previous and they were seen as quite ground-breaking due to their mixed-race members. They had played over two hundred shows already in their short career and had even appeared on the TV show 'The Generation Game'* , which had been their one chance at prime-time TV so far.

"Bravo, bravo!! More. Encore!" bellowed Kang, in near perfect English; his Chinese accent having almost completely disappeared over the course of his studies and his now permanent residence in England.

As the band struck up again, letting rip with a pounding beat that got more of the attending crowd up on their feet, Kang picked up his cane and began to mingle with the attendees once more, covering all the ground-floor of Whitchitley Hall. As he slowly passed from man to woman to man - lingering a little longer with the women - he spoke to most of the guests, 'chit chat' and small conversation - but enough to make the people at the party feel appreciated and feel honoured to be there and to have met the man himself.

Then with a sudden bang and the power went…

Everything was deathly silent for a moment, as all the guests stopped what they were doing - mostly talking and dancing – and turned to each other, faces lit in the illumination from the moon that was shining in through the large open windows on the veranda.

"It's ok, my people will get this sorted very soon," shouted Kang across the murmurs and mumbles of the shadows and figures in the semi-darkness, as he shouted orders loudly in near perfect Russian to his bodyguards and in rapid Cantonese to his servants.

The glasses could still be heard 'clinking' as the guests continued to drink and make the most of the party - which had now been cast into darkness. The only other noise was of the servants running to sort out the power-cut and restore the sound, the lighting, and the security system, plus the bodyguards – all female – making a circle around Kang, to protect him from any unwanted well-wishers in the dark.

"*Kang, you bastard...*'

Came the angry scream in the dark, somewhere in the vicinity of the marble staircase. All his army of female bodyguards closed ranks, spinning around in unison, to face the staircase and the lone screamer.

"If people knew what you were up to, they wouldn't come to your lavish parties and give you the time of day. If people knew the 'real, you' they would avoid you like the plague and come nowhere near this den of iniquity." Screeched the woman, who was clearly obsessed with Kang and not at all happy with his 'exploits'.

The 'security circle' wrapped around Kang all drew their weapons – Russian Makarov pistols – preparing for any chance of action at the now suddenly silent party. Kang had assembled an elite squad of bodyguards who had all been trained in the Soviet Union and defected to the west 'en masse', having been contacted via the Russian underground, that vacancies for close protection were going to be available to provide support for a high-flying Chinese businessman, who would pay very well and that was all that they needed to know.

The eight women originally had come to England just a little over eighteen months ago in a small fishing vessel. Setting sail from their hometown, the port of Murmansk – the largest city north of the Arctic Circle - they had sailed around Finland and Norway and headed to the English shores, landing in Felixstowe late at night. They had been collected by more of Kang's security team and transported – under cover of darkness – back to Whitchitley Hall, where their background checks had been verified and they had been briefed on the full nature of their new employment and then they were in the employ of the 'Kang Dynasty' and were known by their '*hit squad*' team name – M.D.S. (Murmansk Death Squad).

As the seven remaining members of the M.D.S. formed a tight barrier around Kang, each with their pistol aiming in the area of the staircase, they stood, awaiting further ramblings from the screeching woman or direct orders from Kang as what action to take next.

"I have a gun myself you know, you crazy fukka…"

The mystery party guest smugly hollered, as she ascended the staircase, walking slowly down towards Kang under the cover of near darkness. Only occasional glimpses of her were seen as the moon shone out from behind the clouds, like a naughty schoolboy spying on the girls in the girls changing room. The light then briefly shone on the weapon she was carrying in her arms, an MP5 – a German 9x19mm Parabellum machine pistol manufactured by Heckler & Koch, capable of taking out all of M.D.S. and Kang, if only she had fired first.

"Take her out, *NOW*" came the direct orders from Kang, in the centre of his 'security blanket' of Russian squad members.

With that the slugs hit the woman in rapid succession, hitting her body with a bone shattering velocity, just as she struck the bottom step, falling forward into the hallway/ballroom area, a spray of blood and teeth flinging itself across the floor, as she face-planted the marble, her nose slipping sideways across her face on impact, a pool of deep red blood pooling out around her head where she lay.

The M.D.S. ran towards the woman and surrounded her, kicking her MP5 into touch and far away from her reach, it skidding across the shiny marble floor and coming to a rest near the open doors to the ballroom.

Several women in the crowd screamed as the lights suddenly came back on, with a bright flash, stunning all the party guests and lighting the room up like a 4th of July Parade. With gunshot fumes and whisps of smoke hanging in the air and blood pooling under the body, several of the female party goers dashed across the floor to see the woman and as they did, she looked up, from under a mass of dark brown curls and spat out the words from her blood drenched lips –

"Get Moist…"

Chapter 1: 'Alligator Man'

'Aztec Chocolate Bar'

Similar in both size and shape to the Mars Bar, the Aztec chocolate bar was a short-lived success, lasting only 11 years in total.

Tasting like a sweeter version of a Mars Bar, it was released by Cadbury's as a direct competition to its adversary in 1967.

The lavish advertising campaign - filmed on location in Mexico - featured several Aztec pyramids, which were mostly used for ritual sacrifices. The only things missing from the adverts were the rivers of bloody plasma flowing down the sides of the pyramid steps; whoever thought this was a good advertising campaign for a chocolate treat had not thought it through and was not considering that the sweets were made originally for children.

Why would you feed your children delicacies that were based around sacrifice, murder, torture, and blood?

Taking that all into account, the chocolate bars were incredibly popular if only for a brief time.

Also note, the bar was called Aztec, due to the Aztec people in Mexico being the ones who discovered chocolate in 600AD.

By 1978 - like the people - the Aztec bar had become extinct, though it was released later again as a special edition in a following decade, to eventually disappear once more at the sacrificial alter of the God of Cadbury.

******

Tonight in the Golden Palace was like any other. A mix of punters and staff, but tonight unlike weekends it was mostly the staff who were outnumbering the clients in attendance, mostly due to it being a quiet weekday and therefore not one of the most popular evenings at the venue.

The club had been open in Soho for over seven years and had been under the same management since the initial launch. The 'dancers' came and went, though the ones that were employed there now had been working at the venue on a regular basis for the last three years, which was unusual. All the ladies and the staff that ran the venue were like a family. They were always looking out for each other, being considerate to each other's feelings, yet still taking care of business.

The venue, though trying to be 'classy' was still a little on the tacky side. The paint, though not peeling yet, was only a few strip shows away from flaking onto the floor and the gold paint, though not too gaudy, screamed cheap and sleazy, not posh, and classy, which was the theme that the owners had tried to go for when they opened the venue in 1963.

There was an overall smell of disinfectant that hung in the air, like the toilets at Butlins – but unlike the holiday camp, this was to clean the floors in the peepshows, that were also part of the venue. Once an hour one of the building team, but usually Bungalow Bill – so named because he had nothing upstairs – would go into each of the peepshows, five cubicles in a row and swab down the decks – cleaning the vinyl floors of any spilt bodily fluids and sometimes there was a lot. They had installed the vinyl flooring in the last year as the carpet had become so sticky and however much you '*mop and bucketed*' the carpet, it was always the same and your shoes would stick to them, trying to ease your footwear off your feet.

There was a low misty haze of cigarette smoke across the whole of the club's dancefloor at this time, which made it difficult to see what was happening on the stage - which was at the far end of the club, at the opposite end to the bar and past all the tables and chairs set up for the punters.

On the stage, one of the dancers - Katerina Ooglestop - was strutting her stuff and gradually peeling herself out of her clothing and getting down to her silky underwear. Her deep red/ginger hair tossed and turned, as she spun around to the sounds pumping out of the inhouse speaker system, her head moving in rhythm to the current tune being played.

As she stood there, gyrating to the music in just a bra and panties a member of the audience - one of the few screamed –

"Get them off you dirty bitch, get your kit off!" and with that he was pounced on. Mere seconds later, the bouncers appeared at his table and told him to behave himself and not to drink any more or else he'd be removed from the premises sooner than he'd wanted to be and before the show finished. Curly Hamilton and Something Fingers were both the door staff and the security for the venue and due to being both over six foot each and weighing in over 240lbs of mostly muscle, they very rarely had any trouble. A look and a few kind words in the ear of a punter and they would behave themselves for the rest of the evening, no more shouting, no more being rude and no more abusing the strippers.

Not fazed by any of this Katerina carried on with her stripping.

It was usual for this time, late at night, to get the weirdo's and the oddballs in and Katerina had had her fair share of them. There had been one time when she had been stripping on stage and a guy had got up and decided he was going to dance with her, strutting his stuff on the small round stage. As the rather curved, rotund gentleman began to take off his clothes the bouncers – still Curly and Something – had moved in from the back of the club and headed straight for the stage. Before he even had a chance to remove his sweaty pants, he was being manhandled out of the club to the tune of 'The Theme from Shaft' by Isaac Hayes.

This performance might have been a problem to other

performers, but to Katerina it was nothing. It was just a run-of-the-mill job and these kinds of things always occurred late at night, especially when you were a seasoned pro at the stripping game and it came as second nature, when you worked like this day in and day out.

Having the security at hand though was a bonus; if the security weren't there it would've been up to the singer or the comedian to intervene and remove people from the venue - but the security were the ones who really were worth their weight in gold and kept the club running, the punters paying and the audience mostly behaving themselves.

If it wasn't for the security staff on the doors and in the club the place would have been a nightmare, with people trying to get away with not paying for the expensive drinks and trying to get out of coughing up for the strip booths and the private shows. With the alcohol being marked up in price, sometimes by up to 80% more than pub prices, there were always people trying not to pay, people trying to get away without spending anything or else they'd be trying to negotiate a discount on their sometimes-extortionate bar bills.

In the back room of the venue, Biffo McGuire, the club manager – sweaty and short with a greasy black comb over - was counting the day's takings and bagging it all up and putting it away in the safe, all the £10 notes bundled up in £200 wads. It had been a good day and Biffo was incredibly pleased how much they had made considering it was quiet.

"It's absolutely dead out there, any chance we can close up soon Boss?" asked Everard Koch the comedian and compere between acts. Everard had been at the club since it had opened and spent his time introducing the girls, telling mother-in-law jokes between the strippers, and still telling his wife that he was working at an all-night garage, which was becoming less and less believable as the years passed by and he still couldn't drive or repair their own car to save his life.

"Give it another thirty minutes and we'll lock the doors up. Who's on now?"

"Katerina, she's nearly in the buff, and so she'll be off within a few minutes, plus it's dead out there now."

Biffo nodded to himself and Everard, he was looking forward to getting home as it had been a long day and Mrs. McGuire hated it when he arrived home when she was just getting ready to go to work in the morning.

"Well, it's 4:15am now, can you see who's upstairs in the tearoom and which girls are already asleep? I think that most of them are still around and they're waiting for Mel and Memory to come back.

"Will do Boss, I know that the maintenance staff all shot off around three hours ago, so there's only the 'ladies', me, Minky, Curly and Something, plus Nat is doing to his closing song in approximately five minutes or so."

As Biffo began to close the safe door, he gave Everard the thumbs up over his shoulder and his compere headed back out of the office to check the rooms upstairs.

******

The gentle breeze was darting around the back lane behind the Golden Palace Strip Club like a Chinese dragon, which was quite appropriate given the proximity of the club to China Town, only a few blocks away, flying from bin lid to beer can, delving into every crisp packet, Aztec chocolate bar wrapper and chip paper.

The silence at the rear of the club was deafening, it was so unlike any other area in London, and it was only when the sleek black vehicle turned in to the lane and pulled up behind the venue, that the deathly silence was broken and as the vehicle came to a stop, all was then quiet once more.

The doors slowly opened on either side of the vehicle - well-oiled doors that made little to no sound, adding to the silence once more. The two women - all in shiny black leather - slipped out and shut both the doors, which made a dull 'new car thud' as they shut tight, and the lane was fell into silence once again.

Walking up to the rear exit of the club, with a large sports bag each, they pushed, and it was not locked, their luck was in. As they went through, they closed the solid wooden door behind them, which shut with a reassuring click.

The area in the back lane was silent for just a short five minutes and then the two women in black came back out the door – without the bags they'd gone in with – and fixed a large and hefty padlock on the door, clicking it shut as they made secure the exit from the club, no one would be using this way out tonight or possibly ever again.

They both re-entered the car and left silently at speed, heading in the direction of Piccadilly Circus and the busier areas of London and beyond at night.

Inside the club, the two large sports bags sat either side of the gas pipes – the main supply to the building

- that entered the club from the courtyard area. The large, flanged pipes came up from beneath the ground and went in at right angles to the wall; a silent, but deadly, invisible killer.

******

The air was still and silent all over London.

It was already 4:30am in Soho and many of the revelers from

the lively night before had gone home, leaving the streets bare and empty - only the rubbish blowing around quietly in the breeze was keeping the beggars and vagrants' company, as they huddled up separately at various locations on the street – all avoiding each other, but totally aware of their 'brothers in rags', just in case another one tried to rob them.

The odd rat could be seen scurrying from left over chip wrappers to half eaten piecrusts and even they seemed bored with their lot as well. Two of the sleek and greasy black vermin fought over a discarded piece of pancake roll and as they did the wind began to pick up, blowing yesterday's newspapers, carrying yesterday's news, around in the streets, taking to the air like cheap kites, soaring and dipping and diving on the breeze.

Within minutes the silence in Soho was filled with rustling as the papers flew about, caught on the breeze and almost waving at the roads below them as they tossed and turned in the constantly increasing gusts of wind.

Then silence…

The streets of Soho were still once more as the wind dropped as suddenly as it had previously picked up and all the swishing papers seemed to hit the pavement in unison, almost like an organised 'ensemble ballet move'.

The streets were bone dry, which for July was unusual, though rain was forecast for the coming weeks, torrential at times and heading in from Europe, where they had received the brunt of the bad weather for the last month.

A car turned the corner into Wardour Street, the 8-track inside blaring out Elton John's 'Tiny Dancer', which echoed around the roads, bouncing off the walls and shop fronts, as the window on the driver's side of the car was wound slightly down.

As the car drove away into the distance, the streets were quiet once more. The only sound in the deathly still, was an old tramp snoring loudly in the doorway to the Intrepid Fox public house, comfortable in his place for the night - hunched up against the wooden frame, his coat wrapped around himself, and his woollen hat dragged down lopsidedly over his eyes, to keep out the intrusive light from the overhead streetlamp.

Then - as if by a premonition or perhaps just a heightened sense of smell - all the rats in the vicinity left en masse; heading down drains, through cracks in the woodwork of some nearby doors and others just scurrying off down the street. They could sense something was about to 'go down' that no one else in the area could, especially the vagrants who continued lying drowsily in doorways, oblivious to what was just about to take place.

And then it happened...

'KAAAAAAABOOOOOOOMMMMMMM!!!'

An all-mighty explosion rocked the foundations of all the nearby buildings and a huge wall of scorching flame shot skywards, the vagrants and beggars all jumped to their feet as they were showered from head to toe in tiny shards of sparkling glass.

Billowing clouds of toxic fumes spread out, enveloping the building that was on fire - the Golden Palace strip club - and the sky around Soho was lit up like 'Bonfire Night' or the '5th Of July' celebrations in the States, as the inferno began raging with an intensity that could be felt on the opposite side of the road and even further down the street.

Three of the homeless people were already screaming in pain, as blood ran in spidery rivers down their faces, where tiny needles of glass had punctured their skin, embedding themselves deep into their exposed flesh. Two of the other tramps -who'd been sleeping behind an industrial bin and had been shielded from the blast - ran to them to help and try to stem the blood flow.

The scene in the street was chaos, the heat was intense from the building, which was still glowing like a Roman candle and one of the vagrants was screaming.

Chapter 2: 'Young Hearts Run Free

'Power Cuts Galore...'

In the UK during the early '70s there were times when the homes across the country were plunged into a darkness that made life an interminable hassle for parents, but an ongoing adventure for children. Sitting around in their homes with candles for lighting and gas ovens for heating, families struggled through the dark evenings, looking to the daylight as a relief.

If your cooker was electric, then gas camping stoves were the order of the day, struggling to cook family meals on equipment best suited for heating up beans and soups at Glastonbury Festival, under the poor lighting emanating from the multi-packs of standard white candles.

The power cuts were taken as a direct result of the miners and railway workers strikes and could last in the worst situations up to 9 hours at a time.

Three day working weeks were also introduced by the Edward Heath Conservative led government at the time to try and save electricity consumption. These working week disruptions affected all but essential businesses, though these were eventually lifted on 7th March 1974.

******

Within only a few minutes, three police cars and two ambulances arrived in a screech of burning rubber and wailing sirens. The police dived out of their cars and the ambulance crews clambered out of their vehicles and began to assess the situation, just as two fire engines came around the corner – sirens on full -ready to tackle the blaze.

The Chief Fire Officer had seen several fires like this before and knew what had happened straight away.

"It's a gas main that's blown," said the fireman as he watched his teams preparing to douse the flames, their hoses already unfurled halfway along the street.

"We need to isolate the main gas supply and then we can tackle the fire and stop it spreading", he said, his brow furrowed from the worry of another extreme fire on his watch, the second one this year; his first had been a major blaze very close by in China Town and many of the shops along one of the roads had been destroyed. The stores still hadn't been returned to their former glory due to the families being too poor to afford adequate insurance and so their properties could not be rebuilt, due to insufficient funding available for the major structural repairs that were required.

Within a few short minutes, firemen in asbestos/flame-retardant fire-fighting gear had located and turned off the gas supply for the street and the intensity of the flames had died down slightly and with the hoses trained on the upper floors of the Golden Palace, the fire began to decrease, and the fire fighters halted the flames from spreading along the street, from one building to the next. The water cascaded down through the floors, eventually dousing out the still raging fire on the ground floor, the windows at the front all cracked and the wooden frames damaged beyond repair, as the water drained out into the street. The paramedics tended to the bleeding homeless people and under the strip lighting in the ambulances, attempted to remove most of the tiny shards of glass from their exposed flesh. Luckily for the vagrants, the fact that the three of them had been well wrapped up, there was a lot less uncovered skin than there could have been, especially if the explosion had taken place earlier in the day, when the weather would have been warmer, and they would have had looser and less clothing on.

"We're going to need to get you all to the hospital to clean you up completely", said the Senior Paramedic - the three down-and-outs nodding in unison as they were feeling lucky to be alive, the explosion having sobered them up and cleared their heads of the alcohol induced fug of the earlier evening.

As the ambulance crews gradually tidied up their workspaces and the drivers climbed back into their seats, the ambulances prepared to leave, heading for the nearest hospital A&E, which was St. Thomas' Hospital on Westminster Bridge Road, only a short drive away.

As the medical teams left the area, the fire crews carried on tackling the blaze, as the flames gradually died down and the whole area was covered with a 'steaming mist' caused by the heat and the water. It was hard to see what was happening nearby and the firemen prepared for their inevitable final part of their job, the exploration of the building, checking for corpses and looking for the cause of the fire, if they were able to determine a reason for the accident.

It was obvious to the Chief that the main cause of the devastation was the gas explosion, but what had caused it? Gas mains don't just tend to blow up of their own accord, especially in the middle of the night, especially with the power-cuts that they were experiencing on a weekly basis now.

The Chief was Byron Read, he was living now with Nancy Redmond, but things weren't good. He worked long hours, and she was a Nurse at Old Church Hospital in Romford and due to her shift patterns as well, they found little time to spend together. They had been together for over three years, but as their work positions had changed – they had both been promoted – they saw less and less of each other, they were like the proverbial '*ships passing in the night*' and being a couple was becoming more and more difficult, as they were gradually drifting apart.

Standing staring at the building, watching his crew gradually undertake their positions, as they steadily moved closer to the frontage, Byron began to daydream – which in his highly significant position was not a good idea. He was tired, he was thinking about ending his relationship with Nancy, due to the complications with never spending quality time together.

As the thoughts spun around in his head, his crew toiled at getting the remainder of the blaze under control. The flames were now almost non evident, and the suited crew were getting ready to make their first access of the building checking for any causes of the fire and any casualties.

Then there was a scream…

"AAAAARRGGGGGHHHHHHHHHHHHHHHH!!!"

Byron spun around to see a woman literally shaking in the street and screeching like a banshee at the top of her lungs, as her heavily painted nails pointed at the building.

"NOOOOOOOOOOOOOOOOOOOOOOOO!!!"

The look of total desperation on her face becoming more apparent as the floods of tears began to fall from her deeply mascaraed eyes, leaving trails of blackened smudges, rivers of make-up rolling down her cheeks and her neck. She looked like a female Alice Cooper impersonator with the smudged eye make-up and her huge breasts.

Byron watched as the girl continued screaming, shaking uncontrollably as she waved once more at the building.

The police who were in total control now, ordered her back

from the already cordoned off area and she stood nearer to Byron, clearly very distraught, in total shock and inconsolable.

Moving towards her, the girl continued crying. Heavy sobs and deep breath's alternating, as she tried to calm herself down, teetering on the brink of hyperventilating.

"Are you ok Miss?" asked Byron, leaning in towards her, making eye contact and trying to calm the situation down.

As she stood on the side of the street, her feet tapping away on the paving stones, Byron stared at her, rivulets of tears still running down her face, making trails through her make up and darkly dribbling down her neck.

She was clearly still very distraught, and he had to find out what was up.

As he walked closer to her, he realised what an attractive woman she was. From her long silky dark hair to her slim figure, she was amazing - in the eyes of Byron - but the thing that stood out most about her were her massive breasts.

It was then that Byron realised where she'd come from and where she was going.

She was being stopped from heading back to the source of the fire - she was a stripper at the club that was currently in the process of burning to the ground, destroyed beyond recognition and never to be the same ever again.

"Excuse me Miss but do you know what's happened here?" Byron asked her, as her puppy dog eyes looked up at him.

"I've been away for the evening and now I've come back to this. I can't believe what's happened - all my friends are in there, but I can't bear to think about it" she replied, rubbing, and dabbing at her eyes with an already soaking wet tissue.

Byron looked at her, he was right she worked or at least once upon a time had worked at the building, but he needed to know more about her.

"Is there anything else you can tell me?" She lifted her chin up and looked him straight in the eyes and said -

"I'm Moist..."

Chapter 3: 'Sugar Baby Love

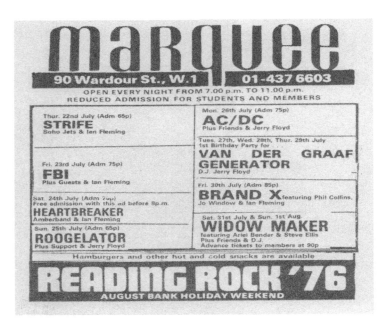

'The Marquee Club'

The Marquee Club was opened originally in 1958, but in the mid '60s moved location to Wardour Street in the middle of Soho, London, and that's where it stayed until it closed and moved to Tottenham Court Road after it was sold in 1988.

The club was run by Harold Pendleton, and he was an avid jazz fan, who went on to set up the National Jazz Festival, which eventually became Reading Rock Festival and then the Reading and Leeds Festival, with the same line-up playing on different days over the two sites.

During the 1970's the venue played host to many future stars from Adam Ant to The Jam to Joy Division to the Cure and Dire Straits. All the 'up and coming bands' wanted to play there and bigger bands wanting to perform a more intimate gig wanted to appear there as well. Even Queen, David Bowie and Status Quo graced the boards at the tiny club, with a 700-person capacity.

******

M y name is Melanie Moist", she sobbed as she told Byron her name, for that was what she was called *'Melanie Moist'* and even though she had only worked there for 18 months, she was still the longest enduring stripper at the Golden Palace strip club in Brewer Street, Soho and now she had joined the shuffling ranks of the recently, involuntarily unemployed.

"I work in there," she blubbed, pointing a delicately manicured finger once more at the smoldering wreck, that was once her place of employment, her only means of paying her bills - now a mess of charcoal, exposed angled beams and broken glass.

"Worked in there…," she corrected herself, as she continued to stare glassy eyed at the remnants of her ex-workplace.

******

Melanie had started work at the strip club quite by accident. She had arrived in London, with no job and no money, staying initially at her 'Nana's' a short train ride away in Romford. If she caught the fast train from Liverpool Street, it only stopped at Stratford and Ilford before pulling into Romford a short while later. If she accidently or unfortunately caught the 'slow train', it stopped at all the stops in between, including Chadwell Heath, Goodmayes and Seven Kings.

With the proximity to London, Melanie had thought that it would've been easy for her to pick up some work, casual or otherwise. She imagined that it wouldn't have taken long for her to get a job at one of the major stores on Oxford Street – she had plenty of retail experience – but it just wasn't meant to be, the jobs she applied for, seemed to go to people who had just left school and so the employers could employ them cheaply and pay them in buttons; Melanie needed a fairly reasonable wage so that she would be able to move into her own flat and become independent, but it seemed to take a lot longer than she had expected.

She made a claim a few weeks after arriving in Romford and was now officially 'on the dole' – the money wasn't great, but it gave her something to keep her going, a financial cushion and she was glad that she even had that, at least.

Being 'youngish' and still full of the joys of spring, Melanie would get the train into London most weekends and occasionally weekday evenings as well, and head into Soho to soak up the night life and hang out in the pubs and clubs, drowning her sorrows at still being without a job.

It was on one of these weekends that she was hanging out in Soho, at 'The Ship' on Wardour Street, and a guy who was sitting next to her at the bar, struck up a conversation.

"I seem to see you in here every night?" he began, raising his glass in a non-formal kind of salutation.

"I'm not here all the time you know, though I wish I could be!"

"Whereabouts do you work? Around here?" he asked, raising an eyebrow, and turning around to face her full on his seat.

"I'm still between jobs, as they say," Melanie replied, trying to smile, though the lack of constant funding for her trips out were using up most of her 'dole money' and Nana had to subsidise some of her evening excursions.

"I'm looking for someone."

'I bet you are,' she thought to herself as she moved a little in her seat, starting to feel uncomfortable. Her Nana had warned her about men like this trying to pick up young girls in bars, pubs, and clubs in Soho, but would she listen? Would she hell!!!

"I work at the Marquee Club* a few doors away and I'm looking for someone to man the cloakroom daily or at least when the gigs are on. The money isn't brilliant, but it will help I'm sure until you get a new job?"

"Oh my god!!! Of course, I'll take it. I thought you were just a pervert who hits on young innocent women?" smiled Melanie, already regretting her choice of words, as they left her mouth – she did have a habit of not putting her brain into gear before she opened her lips, but he seemed to like what she said and was already laughing his head off, with his loud guffaws attracting many glances from around the pub.

"My name's Harold, I run the club, you're hired."

With that Melanie began her job checking in people's bags, coats, and hats, at one of London's coolest music venues.

For several months she was part of a team that was considered integral to the venue's success. She ended up being on first name terms with many of the bands that came through the venue, from Caravan to Pink Fairies, from Mungo Jerry to Slade and not to forget a 'one off' performance by the Rolling Stones.

One night as she stood on the door to 'her cloakroom', collecting people's coats and issuing grubby ticket stubs, a guy came through late on in the evening, when the concert had already begun. As the music from the band filtered through the constantly opening and closing swinging doors, a short, balding man with a jet black 'comedy combover' walked up the hallway towards the cloakroom and just stopped, staring at Melanie.

"Can I help you?"

Still staring at her he said, "I have a proposition for you, if you'd like to give me just five short minutes of your time."

The little man went on to explain that he was a local businessman and that he ran a club with a late-night licence, only a few minutes' walk away and that he was always on the lookout for appropriate people to join his staff and become part of the team. He went on to explain that they were like a little family, and everyone was very friendly, and they all looked out for each other. He then went on to explain the position to her.

"Well, the money is pretty good, and you can add tips on to your salary as well, depending on how pleased the punters are with the performance."

"Performance?" asked Melanie, raising an eyebrow as she checked in another coat from a late comer to the club.

"Can you dance?"

Now a little confused - as she handed out another ticket for the leather jacket that had just been deposited – she raised her eyebrow and the penny eventually dropped.

"You're offering me a job as a stripper?"

"I prefer to refer to my performers as exotic dancers, it sounds much classier, and keeping in with the overall ambience of the club."

"You want me to dance naked for perverts?" said Melanie, hands on hips and with a look of total shock on her face.

"Think of it more as a performance and overseeing your own future, a way to fulfil your destiny. You can earn a lot of money in this game, and you certainly have the looks – and figure – that would be incredibly popular amongst our clientele. You're a beautiful woman and are wasted working here handing out tickets and collecting peoples clothing – no one wants to see you doing that for the rest of your life, let alone yourself, I'm sure. The future could be so much brighter for you."

You could almost see the cogs spinning in Melanie's head, as she thought about the lewd proposal. She wasn't shy, but would she be able to dance in the 'all together' in front of a group of unknown strangers? But the money would be a big bonus and she didn't want to live with her Nana forever – her own place, a private girly pad, sounding very appealing, especially if she could get a place close to the centre of London.

"Tell me more about this job," she continued and Biffo McGuire went on to tell her all he could about the Golden Palace.

He told her about the shifts, the number of performances she would be required to do and all about the staff. He explained in detail the rules of the venue and how they were covered by strict health and safety guidelines, which made everything secure and how the girls were protected by the security staff who were also in attendance every night. Biffo talked of the other girls and how they all looked out for each other and covered each other's performances if anyone was ill or just not feeling up to it that evening. He spoke about the additional members of the team, from the musicians and comedians to the building maintenance team and the door staff who also acted as the main security team for the building.

The more that Biffo spoke to Melanie about the proposition, the more enticing and interesting it sounded and within a few more meetings and chats over a few weeks, Melanie was persuaded to take up her new employment at the Golden Palace as a bona fide stripper or exotic dancer as he kept calling them.

So, within the month, she had moved out of her Nana's and taken up residence in the Golden Palace, living above the property, making immediate friends with all the girls, and putting money away for her 'flat fund'.

But that was then…

******

The large panelled main doors at the front of the building were hanging off their hinges, tilting forwards into the street, looking like they'd never be able to fit back together again, the red paint had already bubbled and pocked where the heat had taken its toll. The top two floors of the building appeared to be completely gone and the three-story structure was now more like a chargrilled bungalow, the shortest construction in the street.

Where once before it stood tall and erect - a proud monument to the sex industry - it was now a flaccid burnt-out shell and no number of sexual encounters that had taken place within over the years, were going to save it.

The two fire crews were still training their hoses on the ground floor of the building, and it seemed that they were finally getting the blaze under control.

Water was gushing out of the two high power hoses and the flames in the structure seemed to be gradually diminishing. All that seemed to be coming out of the building now was clouds of hot steam, where the water had cooled down the flames, and billowing clouds of smoke - the less damp areas of the building were still glowing a little, but the flames had been vanquished, bringing some normality back to the scene in the Soho street.

"Oh no" she suddenly screamed, raising her hands to her mouth in shock, as if she had just remembered something of vital importance, the reality of the situation spreading rapidly across her tear-stained face.

"Did my friends all get out of the building safely?"

Byron stared at her, putting an arm around her shoulders to try and calm her down, before delivering the sadly inevitable news.

"We've seen no one."

Then the floodgates opened full blast, the tears cascading down her already wet and shiny face, heading down to her dampened, half buttoned silk blouse.

Melanie began to shake uncontrollably as her sobs intensified and the thoughts of her friend's perishing in the ruins of the establishment where she used to work gradually began to sink in. The shakes increased as the thoughts began to fill her head, she was alone, and her friends were gone.

Byron was a little out of his depth now, as he looked down at the sobbing woman cowering under his arm. The fire service hadn't really prepared him for this kind of situation, and it was at this point that he caught the eye of one of the female victim support officers that the police had sent and called her over.

"Excuse me officer" he called across the street, "this young lady has had a terrible shock and needs to talk to someone. Can you help?" he asked the young officer, hopefully trained to deal with these intense situations on a regular basis.

The support officer crossed the road, her uniform buttons sparkling in the dazzling lights from the fire engines. Elizabeth West has joined the police force at the age of 24 and she was now nearing her 32nd birthday, so she'd already served nearly 8 years for the Met. She was currently single and very career motivated and believed herself to be an excellent VSO (victim support officer) - which was her role of choice now - and her skills had been already recognised by her commanding officer, in her end of year assessments.

With her hair tied tightly in a regulation bun, she looked every part the professional policewoman, as she crossed the road to look after Melanie, taking her out from under Byron's wing.

Elizabeth put an arm around Melanie and led her away to behind the fire engine for a chat, Byron watching them as they disappeared into the distance.

But then Byron had a change of heart and followed the two women and caught up with them behind the vehicle, shielded from the heat still emanating from the smoldering shell of a building.

"Would there have been any people in the club at the time of the fire starting," asked Byron, trying to keep calm, though totally unprofessional - he was more staring at her chest, than taking in her answers.

Melanie shrugged her shoulders.

"It's February, it's a cold night at 5am – where else would they be? All my friends must've been in the building. Their shifts would've ended around 3am and then they would've gone to their rooms to relax and wind down. It's a hard life being an entertainer you know…"

Byron nodded, trying to ooze empathy, like she was oozing sex appeal. He stared at her some more, maybe for too long, as he began to feel embarrassed that he was still ogling her a little too much.

'Focus, focus, focus, on the job, not the body,' he thought to himself, trying not to stare too much.

She took her hands off her hips and pushed them deep into her jacket pockets and stood up as straight as she could, her back clicking in the process.

"I feel like I need to go and have a rest, but I don't know where I can go to now" Melanie said, tears welling up once more.

"Before you go anywhere, we will need a list of who might have been in the building at the time of the fire," said the deep voice from behind her.

Turning around she was confronted with the policeman who'd asked the question.

"Hello Miss, I'm Detective Inspector Gregory Morgan and I just need to ask you a few questions before you will be able to leave. It'll all help the investigation and hopefully make sense of what has happened here tonight."

Melanie stared at the policeman. He was in his early fifties, overweight – bordering on 'morbidly obese', approximately 5' 8' tall, but appearing very well presented in his uniform, all creases in the right places and polished buttons that would blind a Bigfoot at fifty yards in the woods.

She smiled, thinking of all the fun times she'd had in that building; all the ups and downs, all the awkward punters who were grabbed by the bouncers and above all, her memories kept going back to the people she had worked with, who were now no more? Possibly just charred remains in a scorched and seared building.

"Sure, I can give you the names of all the staff that should have been in there after their shift, but could I have a drink of water first please?"

Nodding, the policeman went back to his car that was parked at the side of the road and came back with a plastic canteen of water, passing it over to Melanie.

Twisting the lid and raising the water container to her lips, she gulped down a couple mouthfuls of water, as rivulets dribbled over her ruby red lips, heading southwards down her neck and pooling in her cleavage, glistening in the early morning sunshine.

Both Byron and DI Morgan's jaws dropped, until they both realised that Melanie was staring at them over the top of the canteen, closing their mouths in unison and looking around as Melanie began to speak.

"We were all known by some crazy handles" she began, with Morgan starting to take notes in his notepad, licking the end of his pencil before beginning.

"I never knew any of the girls by their own names, as it was easier and safer to just use our nicknames, that way punters couldn't ask us a girl's name and try to track her down or find where she lived, it was just an unwritten rule."

"OK, so what were the names of the girls who were at the club tonight and why were you not there working?"

Melanie looked at him, tears welling up in her eyes.

"I was at my Nana's in Romford, she's not been well of late, and I had taken a night off to go and spend some quality time with her, she is 90 in a month's time and I'm hoping that she'll make it."

Melanie went on to explain that her Nana had been suffering from some very severe bouts of depression and it was only her friend calling at her house the other day that had shrugged her out of taking an overdose and ending it all. She was very close to Nana and to lose her would be devastating.

Byron stared at her, as the smoke in the air continued to fill his lungs with each carefully taken breath.

"The girls were – Chumpy Tuppence – she's my best friend, Memory Lane, Katerina Ooglestop, Tuna Tunnel, Crusty Bucket, Fishy Waffle, and Ophelia Flange. They were the only dancers that would have been in the building tonight, but there were lots of other people in there too. Including all the male members of the band and the security staff and manager."

Raising their eyebrows in unison at the amusing names, Byron and Morgan awaited the next names of the male staff, as Melanie carried on with her list of missing staff.

"Well, there was Minky Bob, Curly Hamilton and Something Fingers, who all worked the doors, providing the security and keeping myself and the other girls safe. Biffo McGuire was the manager of the club and ran a very tight ship. Nat King Cock was the tribute act, which played every night and Everard Koch, was the comedian and compere who linked the night together, introducing the music, welcoming all the girls on stage, and eventually calling final orders at the bar, at the end of each evening."

"Anyone else?" asked DI Morgan, writing the last of the Cock/Koch's into his notebook.

"The only other people were the support crew, an electrician, a handyman and a plumber, they are Tommy Hawk, Bungalow Bill, and Bognor Philbin" and then she added an afterthought to clear up what she was stating, "I say are and not were as the three of them would not have been working at all tonight as they usually finish at just after 8pm each evening."

"Why do they call him Bungalow Bill, the handyman?" asked the policeman, looking up from near illegible scrawling's in his notepad, with a confused look on his face.

"Because he's incredibly dim, no common sense – he's got nothing upstairs; great with his hands though," she remarked ignoring the briefest of sniggers from the policeman and the fireman, who both coughed at the same time, appearing to clear their throats, but really, just covering up their amusement.

"Well, you certainly have a colourful collection of work colleagues," replied DI Morgan, trying to make light of the situation.

"Had," Melanie corrected him, knowing in her heart of hearts that most of her colleagues - many of whom had been close friends - had died in the fire and it would only be a matter of time before the crews in attendance would be removing the charred remains and identifying the bodies by dental records and any other distinguishing factors.

"Sorry Miss, I stand corrected. Fingers crossed a lot of your friends were able to vacate the building when the fire started and will come forward over the next few hours, though I would've thought they would still be here now, but there appears to be no bystanders apart from the few vagrants that are about now. But like I said Miss, in these situations we do hold out hope for the best results and possibly some of your colleagues left early or weren't working today, but this will all come to light hopefully in the next few hours."

Looking around as he finished speaking, there appeared to be more people on the street now, several people who'd just come by 'rubbernecking' to see what was going on and others who had started to arrive for work in the other buildings on the street; no one seeming to be anything to do with the Golden Palace.

Byron looked at her from as close a distance as he could without coming across as 'creepy'. She reminded him of his sister - though obviously he never had thoughts about his sister like the ones he was having now about Melanie.

"Is there anything I can do to help you now" asked Byron, smiling at her with his eyes, licking his lips as well as he looked at her across the still smoky area of the street.

The smoke was laying low now and resembled a real London 'pea-souper'; it looked like something out of a Sherlock Holmes novel, minus the interventions of Moriarty.

"I need to have somewhere to stay and sort myself out," She replied wiping the tears off her face. It had been a bad night and now she was homeless and feeling hopeless, lost on the streets of London.

Byron looked back at her, it was going to be hard to get this one past his girlfriend, she wouldn't be in a good mood as it was possibly the worst time there had ever been in their relationship, and he was already toying with the idea of bringing a strange woman home to their house?

"Bear with me, I'll speak to my other half about it, to see if you can stay at our place for the night" he replied, getting ready to dash off to find a call box to ring Nancy and explain the complexities of the current situation for the 'ex-stripper'.

"If I could just have somewhere to get my head down for a few hours, it would be appreciated," she replied, smiling through the smudged make up and tearstains.

With that Byron ran off down the road towards the Windmill Theatre where he knew there was a telephone box, leaving Melanie with DI Morgan.

"Well Miss, I'm just going to have a quick wander around and ask few of these 'people of the street' if they saw anything when the building went up in flames or any time before that." And with that he wandered off down the street, nearer the remnants of the strip-club and Melanie ended up standing talking to Support Officer West.

"So, what's it like working in this industry then?" she asked, trying to take Melanie's mind off the fact that all her friends had probably died, in the most horrendous fashion, in a fireball of heat, shattering glass and splinters.

"It's fun most of the time, but you do get the occasional weirdo come in or groups of young guys with their mates, all on a 'stag do' hoping to see some titties and not spend much money – but if they think it's gonna be cheap, they've got that completely wrong," she began, her eyes flitting between the shell of the building and Elizabeth West.

"The prices are all marked up quite clearly on the chalkboard at the bar, but no one ever pays any attention to that, when the girls are dancing. All they want to do is cheer, drink champagne and knock back shorts and flirt with the girls - them flirting back and getting them to drink even more. That's what happens every night and when it gets to closing time that's when we find out that the young guys can either just afford to pay the bar bill or not at all, that's where Minky, Curly and Something work their magic; I've seen my fair share of broken fingers, bruised eyes sockets and split lips – enough to last me a lifetime, but the boys and men still come back, just being more careful the second time around."

Elizabeth smiled, it sounded so totally removed from her own job and anything that she had ever done - or thought of doing – in her own lifetime; it almost sounded like a film, a smutty, but fun 'X rated' film, the kind that showed in the Adult Cinema's that were scattered all over Soho and in the heart of 'Strip-club Land', where the club once stood as a beacon to 'tits and ass'.

"I'm not sure what I'm going to do now?" Melanie continued, the salty tears welling up in the corners of eyes once more. "This is all I've ever known. I help the new girls, I keep the older girls on track and keep the men at arm's length, it's what I do, it's what I've done for ages now – it is what it is."

Footsteps approached them from behind and they turned around to see Byron, back from his jaunt to the phone box.

"Well, I can't get hold of Nancy, she must be still on her shift, but I'm sure it'll be ok if you come back, we've got a spare room after all…" he smiled, already planning his excuses and reasoning behind bringing a stripper back to their flat – a good looking, sexy, large breasted 'youngish' woman, who danced naked for men.

What could go wrong when Nancy eventually came home from her shift…?

Chapter 4: 'Thank You For Being a Friend'

'The Kid's Aren't Alright...'

During the 1970's the sexual revolution had been and gone and there was a whole new feeling around the world, nowhere more so than in England, where perverts abounded and what seemed ok at the time, has since been recognised - and rightly so - as totally inappropriate, scary, and terrifying in later years, when looked back at with hindsight.

All our 'heroes' and TV legends creeped their way around the young adoring population of the UK, preying on the vulnerable, the defenseless and the children and young adults at risk to becoming victims to these dangerous predators.

Gary Glitter was riding high in the charts and molesting people who wanted to 'be in his gang'.

Jimmy Savile was working his way through the attendees at the 'Top of the Pops' studio and Stoke Mandeville Hospital.

Rolf Harris was asking if people wished to see his 'extra leg' "diddle diddle diddle dum" and Cyril Smith MP was just being gross in a larger-than-life kind of way.

******

Once the police had finished dealing with questioning the people who lived 'al fresco' on the streets of Soho, Melanie and Byron were able to leave - heading back to Romford, to where Byron and Nancy lived, quite near to where Melanie's Nana's home was as well.

In the car on the way Melanie was silent.

She was sitting in the front next to Byron, contemplating, thinking about what had happened and where she was to go from here. Her job was over, she had nowhere to live, and she had no income. Luckily for her, she had saved several thousand pounds up already that was 'un-declared' to the Tax Office and the any benefit systems.

She'd have to waste her time going to the 'Dole Office' to make a claim again, something she hadn't done in the last ten years, which was a good thing, a very good thing, but she needed to remember not to mention the undisclosed cash that she had floating around her belongings and not held in any bank accounts. She would have to be very careful and not let slip that on some evenings she had been getting over £50 in tips and sometimes more than that from the more affluent punters.

She was also very worried about attending the Benefit Office - there was nothing worse than the thought of going into one of those bland grey buildings and bumping into one of the bland grey guys who had seen her strip, paying their spare dole money in grubby greasy tips.

******

It had been bad enough when she'd been on a quite frenetic shift one afternoon and had left the club in the middle of the London rush hour, looking to hop on a tube at Piccadilly Circus.

Fresh from a shower, her hair still damp and hanging on her shoulders, but with her make-up already applied - as she always wanted to look her very best, because you never knew who you might bump into.

Squeezing through the hot and sweaty crowds to get onto the tube train and find a seat, she sat down and started reading a discarded newspaper that was lying on the empty seat next to her.

It seemed like the protests against the Vietnam war were in full flow in Washington the day before – over 500,000 people had marched on the capital and there had also been a smaller protest in San Francisco at the same time, but that had still hit around 150,000, so still a sizeable gathering.

As she checked the TV listings for that evening, planning to watch 'Opportunity Knocks' with her Nana and then her favourite 'Bless This House' with Sid James, she noticed that someone was staring at her. Sitting right opposite her was someone that she thought she recognised but couldn't put her finger on it.

She stared at the guy.

He stared back, a cold icy stare.

Young, slim, long black hair – spiky on top, lengthy at the sides and back - and lots of bangles and rings and he was staring right back at her.

And then he winked.

And then the proverbial penny dropped for both of them.

The guy sat opposite her was one of the punters that had been getting his rocks off in the club, only an hour or so before and as she stared at him, he went bright red as he'd just realised where he'd seen her before and spent the rest of the tube journey staring at his nails; it was the longest 30 minutes they had both had to endure and the thought of going to a similar 'stand-off' in the dole office, wasn't her idea of a fun outing either.

******

Then the news came on the cars radio, blaring louder over the sound of the engine and the usual honking of horns in the centre of

London, shaking her out of her daydream, with her ears perking up at the main story.

"NEWS just coming in. There's been a massive explosion in Soho and a 'gentlemen's club' has been destroyed in what has possibly been described as a gas explosion.

We are still waiting for further details, but it has been reported that due to it being a catastrophe of quite a vast magnitude, there may have been several fatalities.

We will keep you up to date on any developments and will be reporting directly from the scene very soon…"

Leaning forward, Melanie flicked off the switch and the car was once again in silence, just the noise of them speeding along the road, avoiding cyclists, and stopping at another set of red traffic lights.

"Sorry, but I couldn't bear to listen to the details again, it's been a bad enough night already."

Melanie flipped down the visor to give her make-up the once over in the mirror and for the briefest of seconds, three pale wan faces looked back at her, not smiling, just acknowledging her from the back seat of the car. The shimmering faces half smiled at her, and she blinked her eyes several times, to make sure that she wasn't imagining what was in the back of the Viva. Spinning around she was met with nothing, just empty seats and no one sitting there at all – but she could've sworn that she had seen a few of her friends or something that resembled them at any rate, a few seconds earlier in a fleeting, bleary eyed glimpse.

"Just hallucinating…" she said to herself, flipping the sun visor back up and scratching her head in confusion.

"What did you say?"

"Nothing," she replied, once more rubbing her eyes, and thinking that she really needed to get a few good hours sleep at the very least, her mind was already playing tricks with her and the less sleep she got, it would only get worse.

"When I said we lived in Romford, we're actually just a little further out in Harold Wood," said Byron as they passed the road junction at Gallows corner.

"We're nearly there, only 10 minutes and we'll be at our place," he smiled, crunching the gears, as his Vauxhall Viva lurched around the roundabout, almost on two wheels, leaving a dirty skid-mark on the tarmac, as an oily patch on the road caused a bit of nervousness for both of them.

"Lucky we 'clunk-clicked' eh?"

"Yeah, thank god for Jimmy Savile," replied Melanie holding tightly onto her seatbelt as if her life was depending on it.

Just over ten minutes later, they were circumnavigating Harold Wood railway station, passing the shops, and turning into the leafy suburbs of Avenue Road.

Pulling up outside a large and neatly presented semi-detached house, Byron parked the car in the driveway, opened his door, walked quickly around the back of the car, and eased the passenger side door open to let Melanie out.

Sliding, slickly and slowly out from her seat, giving Byron a brief glimpse of her stockings as she swivelled around, Melanie rose out of the vehicle, standing on the gravel driveway, looking every bit the Playboy Bunny, she could so easily have been. If she'd put her mind to it on the day that Hugh Hefner had paid a fleeting visit to the club London in the last few years, things may have been so, so different.

As she straightened her skirt back down and ran her fingers through her long wavy dark hair, Byron headed towards the front door and she followed close behind him, her long heels click clacking on the driveway as she moved with the rhythm of a dancing snake, slithering sexily past the bushes and the begonias.

As the sun was rising, the neighbourhood was now slowly waking up and curtains were already twitching as they made their way noisily up the driveway. Miriam the next-door neighbours - who was a quite spritely old age pensioner, with a false leg and a penchant for being extremely nosey - came sleepily out of her door to collect her milk deliver, her eyebrows raising as she watched the sultry harlot in black walking with Byron up the drive to his house.

"Stare anymore and it'd be easier to take a photo and it'd last longer," purred Melanie, flicking her hair back over her left shoulder.

"If only I had a really cheap and sleazy camera to use, it'd be perfect," replied Miriam as she picked up her three bottles of Gold Top and closed the large green front door behind her, just in case there was a 'Humphrey' about.

"Well, ain't she a fucking charmer, this early in the morning?"

With that comment ringing in his ears, Byron shrugged his shoulders as they headed into his house, closing the prying eyes of the world outside, no point in him upsetting the neighbours, as he had done nothing wrong; in fact, Byron was feeling quite pleased with himself, helping a woman in need and not just a needy woman for a change.

Walking down the hallway they headed into the kitchen and as she looked through the double width French windows into a reasonably sized green space, with a couple trees, a large patch of grass and a small pond, she realised that Byron and his elusive 'girlfriend' were fairly 'well off'.

"Nice place you've got here," Melanie smiled as she looked out into the garden, turning around to take in the kitchen, which also was a well-turned-out area, with all the latest hi-tech gadgets.

"And you've even got a microwave! How groovy!!! You're one of the first people I've met who have one - they were all over 'Tomorrow's World' the other week."

Byron nodded and smiled,

"Do you want a coffee?"

"Yes please, no sugar I'm sweet enough," Melanie replied as she bent down to take her shoes off - the heels were making her feet ache, having worn them all day.

'I bet you are,' thought Byron as he licked his lips, turning on the kettle.

Bending over with her back to him, Byron watched - a slack jawed look on his face as she showed her panties and stockings again, in her very short skirt. Byron was entranced and was finding it difficult to concentrate on making the coffee, pouring milk over his hand, as his eyes undressed her, out of what little clothes she was wearing.

As she sat down on a chair at the kitchen table, Melanie turned her head to Byron, smiling through the tears, which were still ever present in her eyes.

"Thanks for this"

"For what?" Asked Byron.

"All of this. Helping me at time when I've got no one else to help me. No job, no friends left and only my Nana to look after me - but she only has a one-bedroom flat in Romford, so it'll be difficult and a bit of a push for both of us."

"No worries, here to help," replied Byron, the thoughts spinning around at a rate of knots at the back of his head were '*what is Nancy going to think about this?*' He still hadn't been able to get her on the phone after all, when he went to the phone box and just took it on his own thoughts to bring her home to his house, blinded by her looks and the fact that she desperately needed help.

Pouring the coffee into two mugs - a 'Jim'll Fix It' and a 'Catweazle' one - Byron walked across to the table putting the one with a close up of Geoffrey Bayldon's face down in front of her.

"Thanks, it's been a bad night, a very bad night."

Byron nodded, thinking it might get a tad worse when his girlfriend got home.

"Do you mind if I take a shower?" Asked Melanie, "me and my clothes are stinking of smoke" she continued, sniffing her hair, and wrinkling her nose up as the smell of burning strip club drifted up her nasal passages.

"Sure, I'll go get you a towel and show you where the washing machine is," and with that Byron headed to the airing cupboard, choosing a large fluffy pink bath towel, and taking it to Melanie, who was finishing off her coffee in the kitchen.

"It's the door at the top of the stairs right in front of you, the shower is above the bath, see you soon."

With that Melanie rose, her ample hips swinging to the tune in her head, humming to herself as she climbed the stairs and went into the bathroom, slamming the door shut behind her.

In the kitchen Byron sat down at the table, contemplating the argument that was most definitely looming on the horizon, then as he heard the click of a key in the front door, he realised that the argument was much closer to impact than he'd originally expected.

"I'm home, thank god," exclaimed Nancy as she walked along

the hallway and into the kitchen. "That was possibly the busiest night we've had for months, casualty was just full of idiots – Old Church can hardly cope at the best of times, but with these crazy nights I feel like giving up and starting a different career!"

"Stripping…?" mumbled Byron under his breath as Nancy carried on with her tirade on the state of the NHS, the youth of today and the lack of staffing.

"And there were so many staff off sick, again!" she continued, not taking any notice of Byron's comment. "And another thing, I literally bumped into Miriam next door as I was walking up the driveway, she was rambling again, I think she's already been on the sherry this morning, but even this is a bit early for her! She said that a prostitute had spoken rudely to her on our driveway, and she was 'aghast' with what was happening to our neighbourhood, I smiled and came in as quick as I could."

"AGHAST," she re-emphasised, tutting to herself and smirking.

Byron nodded and was thinking '*how the hell am I going to explain this one?*' when Nancy left the kitchen and headed towards the stairs.

"I'm going to have to have a shower, it's the only way I feel that I'll be able to relax today," she said as she stormed off up the stairs before Byron even had a chance to explain.

******

Minutes before in the bathroom, a stark-naked Melanie was just heading into the shower, and she was now in full 'soaped up mode'.

She had found some Vosene on a shelf and was lathering her hair up as the suds and the spray from the showerhead cascaded in waterfalls over her breasts, as she hummed away to herself. She found a bath mitt on the side of the bath and with some children's Matey bubble bath, she began washing herself down, vigorously attacking all her skin that still smelt of the smoky residue of the remnants of the venue.

Then it happened.

As she turned around in the bath, the clear shower curtain moving slightly to the side, she realised to her horror that she was not alone in the bathroom

As Melanie looked out into the bathroom, with soapy tits and foam filled eyes, she noticed that several people were standing there staring at her - Chumpy Tuppence, Minky Bob and Nat King Cock, all shimmering and blurring in the steam of the bathroom.

Melanie rubbed at her eyes to clear the remainder of the shampoo from them, realising that all her friends were gazing back at her, as clear as day.

"Jesus Christ, what are you all doing in here? I thought you'd all been killed in the explosion?" she said, not wondering for a moment, how and why they were all in Byron's bathroom and why they were all watching her shower.

They all looked at each other, Minky Bob nudging Nat King Cock and saying, "You've missed a bit," to Melanie as she reached for the towel to cover up her nakedness.

Then Chumpy Tuppence piped up.

"Well Mel, it's a little hard to explain really, but we are actually all ***DEAD***…"

As the words sunk in, the colour drained from Melanie's rosy complexion, the heat from the shower having made her whole-body glow.

And with that Melanie collapsed out of the bath, slipping on the mat, and falling onto the floor, just as the door opened and Nancy came in and screamed.

Chapter 5: 'Move on Up'

A Little Something for the Week-End?

Nothing says the '70s more than chocolate and nothing is more 'memorable' than the long-forgotten chocolate brands and boxes, which bring back so many memories when someone mentions them, and they allow you to recall your childhood and your early/late teens. The chocolatey goodness of the Week End selection box brings back those thoughts of hot summers, Christmas time and maximum high velocity tooth decay. From the chewy sugar-coated enamel destroying Orange Fruit Jelly and the Lemon Slice to the solid Lime Candy and the Montelimar, they were all filled with such memory inducing molar destroying goodness.

It is such a shame that these candy delights were banished into the darkness of the 'pit of forgotten enchantments.

******

S taring in through the door, Nancy blurted out –

"Oh my god, there's a dead prostitute in my bathroom."

Following Nancy into the bathroom and waiting in the doorway, Byron, looked surprised.

", she isn't. She's just a stripper and I think you'll find that she's just fainted," Byron chipped in, from over her shoulder, trying to make light of the increasingly difficult situation. He had followed her as she quickly marched up the stairs like an army recruit - preparing in his mind his story to explain exactly what was happening en route.

Now looking over Nancy's shoulder, he could see all of Melanie's damp body, spread-eagled on the floor, legs akimbo, her boobs hanging towards each shoulder and her lady parts, all damp, dark and fluffy, only half covered by the towel; she was a sight to see, and Nancy caught him taking a gander, his eyes popping out like organ stops.

"Who the shitting hell is this?" Nancy began, her voicing teetering on the edge of maniacal insanity already.

"Miriam is bloody well right; this neighbourhood is going downhill and it's all my boyfriend's fault! Bringing prostitutes home when I'm out of the house on a night shift!!!"

Byron stood in the doorway, hovering - his mind ticking over as to what to say next to try and alleviate the pent-up tension that Nancy was already verbally spewing out across the steamy bathroom.

"No, No, NNNNo," stuttered Byron, still looking at Melanie – this was going to take some explaining.

"OK, I'm waiting! Why is there a naked, unconscious woman on my best fluffy bathroom rug?" she screeched, looking at all the lacy black underwear, stiletto heels, stockings and leopard print clothing strewn all over the floor like there'd been a mini lingerie tornado just east of Romford.

Byron cleared his throat and began his long tale to try and put an abrupt end to his girlfriend's tirade –

"Well, her strip-club burnt down last night and…"

"And we're a new home for waifs and strays or big breasted bouncy strippers, I guess? Silly me, it just seemed that while I was off working my guts out dealing with alcoholics and accident victims, you were back here shagging prostitutes, but I was wrong, you were home here shagging strippers – I stand fucking corrected."

Copping another sideways glance at Melanie, Byron went back to his story, not that it seemed very believable.

"Well, Melanie…"

"Melanie, eh? First name terms, eh? But of course, you would be on first name terms if you were having an affair, it's not like you just met up with each other last night."

Byron tried to half crack a smile and continued.

", we only met in the early hours of this morning. We were called out to a major gas explosion in Soho and Melanie – sorry, Miss Moist – had been off to see her Nana in Romford and so wasn't involved or even injured, in the blaze."

Nancy looked from the stripper on the floor, on her favourite rug, half wrapped in one of her favourite towels that her Aunt Jessica had given them as a 'housewarming' present and turned her gaze back to Byron.

"And I'm supposed to believe this crap?" she replied to his nonsensical tale of slutty fantasy, raising her left eyebrow as she always did when she was doubting his word.

The last time that he'd been on the end of one of her eyebrows heading skywards, was when she had been on another night shift and he had spent the evening and all of the night watching TV and listening to music on his 'stereo system', forgetting to bring in the washing, that was still out on the washing line in the garden, which she had already reminded him to do when she had left for work at 8:30pm that night.

On arriving back home at 7:30am, it had been heavily raining and all the clothes had fallen onto the muddy garden, the washing line having snapped in the storm that took place as he slept on the sofa - several cans of cider empty on the living room floor, a full ash tray and Pink Floyd's 'The Dark Side of the Moon' playing out on the record player. This had nearly been the straw that broke the camel's back – or in this case the Staff Nurses spine - but they were still together - him, her, and her eyebrows - but the comatose stripper on the bathroom floor wasn't helping the situation at all or even bringing them any closer.

"OK, so if this 'fantasy' that you're trying to cover your tracks with is true, why is she here now in our house?"

"Well, she had nowhere to go, and I hate to see a damsel in distress; you know how kind I can be!" Byron smiled, still knowing that huge soapy breasts were laying just three feet away on his bathroom floor. "For god's sake Nancy, all of her friends have been killed and so would she have been, if she hadn't gone to pay that visit to her grandmother last night, the building was completely destroyed and everyone she knows and all her personal belongings with it."

"I know, I did hear it on the news," began Nancy muttering, "but why the fuck did you think it would be fine with me, to bring her back here??? You helped her just because she had big tits I guess?"

"Has she got big tits?" Byron said out loud, whereas he was thinking to himself that he didn't even notice that she had a head for the first ten minutes...

"Oh, shut up and help me get her up," Nancy said as she wrapped the towel around Melanie, helping her into a sitting position just as she began to stir.

"Where have they gone?"

Byron and Nancy looked as other, questioning looks on their faces, trying to make sense of whom she was referring to; perhaps she was suffering from a bang on the head and had concussion?

"Who?" Asked Byron, shaking his head as her eyes began to roll again as she drifted briefly in and out of consciousness.

Melanie with her back against the side of the avocado bath panel still covered in Matey suds, shook her head, just thinking about what she'd said. Had she really seen her friends? But they were all '*DEAD*' weren't they? And to be honest, that was what Chumpy had said, but she was dead as well?

"I'm so sorry, I'm just a little confused," she began, "I thought that there were some other people in here with me?"

"No, love. Only you me and my adulterous husband!!!"

Looking at the woman with Byron - whom she guessed must have been his girlfriend Nancy – Melanie brushed her damp hair out of her eyes, the long dark locks dripping with now lukewarm water.

"I'm Moist," she said, for the second time that day.

"I can see that you soapy bastard, but what are you doing in my bathroom, what are you doing with my husband and what crap are you talking about?" screamed Nancy, the tolls of a busy hospital nightshift taking its toll on her already shattered nerves.

"I'm Melanie Moist, Moist by name and Moist by…"

"I get it, your name is an amusing stripper name blah, blah, blah!!!" shrieked Nancy, every word dripping in sarcasm.

"No, that's me. My mother is Ami Moist, and my father is Richard Moist, it's our family's name; we are the Moist's of Fiddler's Hamlet in Essex, near Epping Forrest."

Nancy laughed and stared at her even harder, not believing a word she said.

"So, your mother is 'Am I' Moist and your father is 'Dick' Moist? I've never heard so much crap in all my life."

"Now you say that I've never thought of their names like that before. That's a real surprise!" Melanie continued, flipping still damp hair back over her shoulders and out of the way as she struggled against the bath to get up.

"What a crock o'shit," replied Nancy, looking at Byron as he stood still in the doorway staring at Melanie as she slowly tried to get up from the bathroom floor, her towel falling off in the process.

Standing naked in the bathroom, Melanie looked to Nancy and smiled, shrugging her shoulders.

"This kind of thing always happens to me," she beamed, Byron laughing as she said it, his eyes bulging as he stared at her, not needing to undress her with his eyes...

"Turn your back, you filthy, filthy bastard," shouted Nancy, as she slapped Byron alongside the head, making him turn around stunned at both the sight of the naked woman in their bathroom and the heavy backhand from his partner – that was going to leave a mark and would take some explaining on his next shift at work.

"Sorry," mumbled Byron with his back to all the 'action' in their tiny, tiled room.

Melanie standing proud, huge breasts bouncing as she rubbed at her shoulders with the towel, stood face to face with Nancy and started to cover herself up and regain a little of her dignity and with it her composure, though in the game that she was in, her flesh was usually on show.

"I'm really not trying to cause any problems for you both," she began, "but your boyfriend has been nothing but the perfect gentleman and everything he has said - and I have also declared - are the god's honest truth. Byron has been nothing but a kind and helpful person to me this evening and I couldn't have wished for a nicer person to help. You really do have a 'keeper' there and I wouldn't treat him badly as he doesn't deserve it."

Nancy looked at Melanie as she began to wrap the towel tightly around herself, her breasts oozing out over the top, like lava escaping a volcano. She then looked back at her boyfriend, who was standing sheepishly on the landing, rubbing his head where she had slapped him. He really was a 'good guy' she thought to herself as she tried to send a tired smile in his direction. Had she been a little too judgmental, perhaps, but she carried on.

"OK, so if I believe you and the more you waffle, the more believable this story of yours seems to sound, what are you planning on doing next?"

Melanie looking more buxom than ever, now that she was slightly covered up, pulled her hair back into a ponytail, with a band that she had retrieved from her handbag.

"If I could just get a few hours kip and then I'll be out of your hair, not that I have anywhere else to go after here though. I'll get the old brain-cells working on a plan of action for where I can stay after I've rested up a bit, it's been a very stressful night," she almost pleaded; she really was at the end of the road for what to do. Moving into her Nana's flat was not really the most appropriate place to go, and a hotel or guest house would cost her a fortune, especially now that she was unemployed and would be needing a job to pay the bills.

Nodding in agreement, Nancy was broken.

She'd had a bad night and all she wanted was to have a rest as well.

So, would it be that bad to allow the stripper – Melanie Moist, of the Fiddler's Hamlet Moist's – to take a few hours of recuperation in one of their spare bedrooms? She thought not – possibly against her better judgement - and nodding her head once more agreed.

"I'm sorry, it's been a very, very long night and when I came home and found you naked on my bathroom floor, what was I to think? I know that Byron is a great guy and if he has offered to let you stay here for a good rest, then how can I say no?"

And with that, Nancy backed down from her previous rant and showed Melanie to the spare bedroom, Byron watching her hips swing from side to side as she headed into the box room at the end of the hall, her towel barely covering her soft and still pleasingly damp extremities. Her legs were slim, but muscular and Byron had now seen all of them, as well as all the rest of her – but it was more enticing to now see her covered up! Funny things strippers, completely naked - not good, partially clad – amazing, he thought to himself as he headed for his and Nancy's bedroom, even allowing a slight chuckle as he walked along the hallway.

"And where do you think you're going? You ain't completely off the hook yet – you still brought a stripper home," exclaimed Nancy as she turned on Byron, the door to the box room now closed.

"You can sleep for a few hours on the sofa and then bring me lunch up at around 1pm, that'll be good for me and the same goes for Melanie, we now have a house guest, thanks to you!"

Nancy turned and went into their bedroom, shutting the door and leaving Byron alone on the landing, he in turn heading back downstairs and taking up residence for the next few hours on the couch.

It had been a strange few hours he thought to himself as he took off his jeans and t-shirt, pulled the throw off the back of the sofa and lay down to get some 'shut eye' before he had to get up.

An incredibly strange few hours…

Chapter 6: 'Shout It Out Loud'

'Help!...It's the Hair Bear Bunch'

Harking from the tail end of the hippy decade and released in September 1971 (but only featuring 16 episodes) 'Help!...It's the Hair Bear Bunch' follows the adventures of three 'hippy' bears in the Wonderland Zoo and their escapades within and outside of their cave – escaping the zoo when they want on their 'invisible motorcycle' – well it is the end of the trippy '60s!!! They also have a luxurious convertible pad in their cave, that was accessed and decommissioned via a switch on the caves wall. The bears fight for their right to party against the Zoo Director Mr. Peevly and his less than intelligent dim-witted zookeeper assistant Lionel Botch.

Hair Bear is the leader of the bears, Bubi Bear is the small assistant and Square Bear is the simplest of the three, but the owner of the invisible motorcycle.

The show was incredibly unsuccessful at the time and was scrapped after the first season as it was deemed to not appeal to children in the way that other Hanna-Barbera cartoons like the 'Flintstones' and 'Top Cat' did.

The cast read like a 'Who's Who' of cartoon voice legends –

Daws Butler voiced Hair Bear – he was also the voice behind Yogi Bear, Huckleberry Hound, Wally Gator, the Funky Phantom and Quick Draw McGraw.

Paul Winchell who voiced Bubi Bear, was also Dick Dastardly in 'Wacky Races' and 'the Perils of Penelope Pitstop', Fleegle on 'the Banana Splits' and even Gargamel on 'The Smurfs'.

John Stephenson featured as the voice of Mr. Peevly but had previously had a recurring role as Mr. Slate in 'the Flintstones' and additional voices across many, many H-B series.

Joe E. Ross starred as Botch and was also the voice of Sergeant Flint in the longer running 'Hong Kong Phooey'.

******

Closing the door to the smallest bedroom in the house and dropping the towel on the floor, Melanie turned to draw the floral, funky designed curtains. Then still naked, lay down flat on her back on top of the bed, her breasts once more heading east and west towards her shoulders, as she made herself comfortable.

'A few hours' sleep and I'm sure everything will be much better and more understandable in the cold light of day,' she thought to herself as she struggled to try and go to sleep.

Just as she was trying to get herself relaxed, she noticed the warmth in the room change a little, shrugging her shoulders as the temperature began to drop, second by second, getting colder and making her skin begin to bump up on her arms and across her chest, her nipples becoming like small pointy - less than lethal – fleshy bullets.

Slowly exhaling, her breath floated like a voluminous cloud of dense smoke, travelling slowly across the bedroom, as the heat emitted by the radiators, began to have little to no effect across the whole room. What was once – only a few brief minutes before – a warm and cosy space in a home just to the east of London, now began to feel more like a scene from *'Ice Station Zebra'*.

And then it happened.

"Mel, open your eyes, we need to talk…"

With her eyes tight shut and gripping the bed sheets with her hands, Melanie already recognised the voice, afraid to open them, as she knew that the person uttering them was well and truly dead, deep-fried to a crisp in the fire at the club.

"Melanie, open your eyes love, we need your help…"

Slowly, very slowly opening her eyes, Melanie looked up to see once more, some of her 'missing' friends - all standing around her in the room – shimmering and almost glowing in the semi-darkness, due to the curtains being drawn and the morning outside being cloudy and dull. They all had a kind of luminosity about them, unlike anything she had seen outside of a Hammer horror film, but at least she knew those movies weren't real, but this was seriously starting to mess with her mental state.

If she was seeing dead people in a room in Essex, had she died herself already? Was this all a dream and she hadn't gone to nana's that night, but instead had died in the all-consuming flames of the Golden Palace as it went up like dried tinder-sticks?

Or was she just losing her mind? The last grip that she had on reality seemed to be slipping away, maybe due to such a stressful evening. It had really been a traumatic few hours and it felt like this was the peak of a tense time of worry, panic, and multiple deaths.

Slowly opening her eyes and peeking out from behind her heavy lids and the false eyelashes that were still partially attached, the aural nightmare became visual as well, just as her ex-best friend at the club spoke up.

"Mel darling, we are all here and we need your help," said Chumpy Tuppence, casting her hands around in front of all the others in the room as if in a formal introduction, but now there were more than ever and certainly many more than there had a been, only a few minutes ago in the bathroom.

All standing around the bed, looking well considering their situation - with their backs to the window - were Chumpy Tuppence, Minky Bob, Nat King Cock, Katerina Ooglestop, Tuna Tunnel, Crusty Bucket, Fishy Waffle, Ophelia Flange, Curly Hamilton,

Something Fingers, Biffo McGuire and Everard Koch – the whole gang appeared to be back in town, in some form or other for possibly one last final show stopping performance?

Unlucky for some, the twelve apparitions and Melanie stood her and the only thing she could do was drag the covers from her bed, wrapped them around herself and sit up, rubbing her eyes, to make the visions go away.

But they didn't go away, they were still there…

"Hello Melanie," whispered Biffo, "What have they done to my club love?" he continued, a look of genuine concern all over his face, as he glinted and gleamed in the partially lit room, his body casting no visible shadow against the walls or the curtains, as were none of the other club workers that were milling around, smiling, winking, grinning, and waving to her, each in turn.

"What's happening to me?" asked Melanie, feeling that she was possibly talking to herself, even though all the visions in front of her appeared to be there and maybe interacting directly with her. She pinched herself

Then Chumpy moved forward, sitting down next to her, the bed moving as her ethereal form left indentations on the candlewick bedspread.

"We need your help; we desperately need your help…"

Chapter 7:

'It Never Rains in Southern California'

'They Are NOT Dolls'

Action Man was released by Palitoy in 1966 and was a licensed copy of the American action figure 'G.I. Joe'. In 1970 the plastic figure gained the addition of 'real' hair – with a flocked velvety feel to it. In 1973 another improvement was made with the addition of 'gripping hands' which were made of rubber and gave a great upgrading, especially for carrying weapons, especially the handguns.

In 1977 four variations of the Action Man figure were released – Atomic Man, Tom Stone, Bullet Man and The Intruder – but none could match the original style design, though there were always variations, including talking Action man, where a cord was pulled from his chest and indistinguishable catch phrases were uttered and the bearded Action Man who fitted in with the Adventurer and the Sailor figures.

******

"Find out who that woman was, how she got into my party and why she was here to try and attack me," he bellowed at the chief of his security team as they nodded and left the room, leaving Sébastien Kang to his thoughts and his sumptuous breakfast in Whitchitley Hall's huge and lavish dining room.

The large, solid oak dining table - with seating for twelve - was laid out with just the one space, set for Kang at 8am on the cold winter's morning.

Sliced Florida pink grapefruit, sprinkled with delicate sugar spirals, freshly percolated coffee imported directly from Colombia, freshly made, and shipped bread from a farmhouse in South Wales and fine Scottish kippers, sent down by overnight lorry from Scotland – these were how Kang started most days and thought nothing of the extravagance and expense of each meal.

Carefully scooping delicate slivers of grapefruit into his mouth, Kang was contemplating his next move and what could so easily have been his last night on the earth, the evening before. Looking out the window over the grounds as he devoured piece upon piece of the fresh fruit, Kang was disturbed out of his thoughts by the arrival of the leader of M.D.S., #1.

"What have you found out? And don't you dare tell me nothing!!!" Snarled Kang, as #1's mouth slowly opened and then closed again, contemplating what she was about to say and hoping to stay on the good side of his fierce temper.

"Well, Mr. Kang, we have found out a little about the woman that tried to disrupt your party and almost end your life."

"Continue…"

Standing in her leather trousers and tight leather jacket, #1 put her hands behind her back as her clothes creaked and squeaked as she moved and prepared to tell Kang the information that the M.D.S. had gathered from their sources since the night before.

"The woman who was terminated at your party was a stripper, working at the Golden Palace in Soho. As far as we are aware, she was known by a pseudonym which was Memory Lane – we have no official name for her and from the information that we have gleaned, many of the strippers who worked at the club used aliases to protect their identity from the punters."

Kang nodded, knowing exactly where this line of information was heading, he sat back in his chair, placing his silver spoon back on the plate, next to the partially consumed grapefruit, the fingers tips of each hand touching each other, almost in the act of praying.

"All of the strippers that were employed at the club appear to have been killed in a ferocious fire, which occurred last night and all the other members of staff – apart from the maintenance staff – were killed also. There appears to be only one person who has not been accounted for and she is also a stripper, the longest and most dedicated of the performers at the venue…"

"What is she called?" snapped Kang sitting forward in his chair and leaning on his cane as he waited patiently for the answer.

"Her name is Melanie Moist," replied #1, pleased with the fact that she herself had found out the identity of the missing member of the strip-club crew.

Kang smiled, his plan was already coming together and the only piece of the jigsaw that needed eradicating was this missing stripper.

"OK, so you know where the girl from last night came from and you finished her, as would be expected by my security crew; but where is this other girl, this 'Melanie Moist'?"

#1 looked at the floor, eventually her head rising to stare Kang in the eyes, his face already knowing the answer that was on its way.

"We haven't as yet been able to ascertain her whereabouts," she replied in answer to Kang's question, him knowing that this was the reply that was almost definitely on its way as she skirted around the subject of the missing Melanie Moist.

"So, what are your plans to find this missing 'exotic dancer'?"

Kang returned the stare to #1, his eyes burrowing deep into her soul, searching for the slightest glimmer of an answer, a plan, a way forward in tracking down the missing woman.

"I have my sources and a couple of M.D.S. out searching now for her. #3 and #7 have been out in Soho this morning questioning people in the neighborhood, scouring the area and exploring all avenues in my investigation, we will find her very soon, I guarantee it."

Kang stood up, the news had put him off his breakfast and he was now more than ready for some clay pigeon shooting on the estate or a workout in the gym to alleviate the pent-up frustration that was already beginning to build inside himself; this woman had to be found.

"Can you assure me that you will find her?"

"I put my team's credibility on it," she replied, then after being excused by Kang, she turned on her heel, exiting the dining room and heading back to the security headquarters on site.

Kang sat back down at the dining table, his back to the window, *'what am I going to do next?'* he thought to himself, who was this woman and where had she disappeared to?

Pouring himself a cup of coffee he began to contemplate the plans for the day ahead.

He would find her; he would eradicate her or else his security team would, she would not prove to be a problem for very much longer. Soon, very soon she would no longer stand in the way of his plan.

*****

Soho was very cold.

The wind was blowing down Wardour Street like it was on a mission to get somewhere important, gusting past the shops, offices and doorways taking all manner of detritus with it on the breeze.

Grit, leaves, and dust blew down the street, dragging

newspapers, fish and chip wrappers and sweet papers with it - Aztec and Texan bar wrappers vied for supremacy on the pavements, flying around each other in a dance of death as they flew in and out of the mini dust bowl tornados.

A large black car - a Ford Cortina Mk III as favoured by Michael Caine in the movie 'Get Carter' - pulled up at the roadside and two women, both in skin-tight, polished slick leather jackets and trousers exited the doors. They locked the vehicle as they left it, just as the cold breeze continued to annoy them and anyone else that was out and about for work or leisure that day.

#3 and #7 stepped onto the pavement, opposite the Hammer Film studios headquarters, just outside the Marquee Club and walked several yards, then crossed the road and slowly made their way past the Intrepid Fox pub, eventually turning into Brewer Street.

In the distance - just opposite the Raymond Revue Bar - they were met with the sight of the shell, which had up until the night before, been the Golden Palace.

There was still a small police presence outside and a large van from the coroner's office was parked up at the curbside, the crew going in and out of the ruins with black zip-up body bags.

There was little of the building left, some of the internal framework was still visible, but the roof and the top two floors were completely gone – the building was decimated. The remainder of the building had been 'fenced-off' to keep treasure seekers - people mostly hunting for scrap copper and lead - away from any possible pieces of evidence that were still there in the ruins of the building. The building was still a potential crime scene, as the police and the fire service were yet to verify the actual cause of the explosion.

Looking at the building #3 and #7 appeared very pleased with themselves, they loved the visual impact that complete destruction caused and if it hadn't been because of the handy-work of #2 - the bomb expert in the team - they would have loved to have been more involved in it themselves. It was unfortunate that many innocent people had been killed in the process - probably torn to shreds and obliterated by the blast but that was life and they'd seen more people die in Russia at the hands of the KGB for much less important reasons and in much worse conditions.

"#2 certainly knows her explosives," said #3 out loud, openly smiling and getting odd looks from passers-by, who were heading to lunch from their office jobs, as it was now just after twelve o'clock.

"She undoubtedly knows what goes where and what does what," replied #7, who wished that she had the bomb making skills of #2, but she was a close combat expert, her experience being in knives - throwing, flicking, slicing, and stabbing - shiny blades were her 'thing'. To be brutally honest, she was equally jealous of #3's skills in ballistics as well, what she could do by throwing or shooting was a skill set to behold and she always hit her target, her aim and success rate was like that of an Olympic athlete.

Looking the building over from as close as they could get to the foundations - there was a temporary security fence up around the perimeter of the club - they both beamed with pride; Mother Russia would be proud of their work and the way that they were teaching the 'capitalist pigs' a lesson in England, as they had been ever since they first arrived to start work for Kang. Their boss was also one for stirring up trouble for Her Majesty, still begrudging the fact that she ruled over Hong Kong, his home city, which he still wished was under Chinese rule, as it deserved to be and hopefully it would be one day again soon. As #3 walked around the fence, her nostrils inhaling the still strong smell of smoke, she watched the four workers from the Central London Coroner's Office, carrying out the first of twelve body bags - which they would eventually clear in the next twenty minutes. None of the body-bags seemed to be that bulky or heavy, thought #3, probably due to the intense heat, that had burnt all the hair, flesh, muscle, and other body parts away to nothing, the bags just containing bones, skeletons of the former workers, she guessed, trying not to get in the way.

"Move along please Miss, nothing to see here," called one of the policemen as the fence was pulled back across the building, as the final body-bag was loaded into the rear of the coroner's van.

"What's happened here?" Asked #3, already knowing the true answer, but not expecting what she was about to hear.

The policeman who was still standing against the fence, went totally against protocol, replying –

"I think it was sabotage Miss, but don't say you heard that from me."

"Sabotage?"

"I think that there is some kind of 'porno turf war' going on. One strip club does better than another, who does better than a sex shop, who does better than the sleazy movie club – there can't be too much money made from the sale of brightly coloured rubber dildos and smutty books and magazines can there? It only takes a matter of time before one boss gets angry with another and then all hell breaks loose, just like you can witness here. But don't say that I said that to you…" the policeman replied, scratching his head, not sure why he'd blurted out what a lot of other people in the local area were already thinking.

Smiling, #3 walked away from the fence and headed back across the now fairly busy street to where #7 was leaning against a lamp-post, smoking one of her 'Belomorkanal' Russian cigarettes; they were her smoke of preference due to being the strongest available in Eastern Europe and also due to being very cheap as well, but they did give are a very husky and guttural voice, which many men – and some ladies – found quite sexy, when you got past the smell.

"That fuzz over there thinks that it's all to do with the sex industry competing against each other, just internal squabbling and taking revenge on each other due to their profit/sales margins – we seem to be out of the picture at the moment, it's all good for us."

#7 smiled, taking a long drag on her cigarette, thick clouds of Russian smoke eventually exhaling through her nostrils and filling the doorway of the local newsagents, just as an elderly lady came out, carrying a bag of pick and mix and that day's copy of the Daily Mirror. "You filthy creature, out of my way," moaned the woman, dressed like she was heading for church in her Sunday best, her hailed piled up on her head like a wonky beehive.

"Do you want to die?" Drawled #7, her husky tones sounding as chilling as they were sincere. "I could slice you up here, take you in to a back alley and gut you like a dirty Siberian Tiger and sell your meat to the local butchers…"

Looking worried the old lady rushed past the two women, bustling straight across the street to the policeman that was still guarding the fenced off strip-club ruins.

"That woman over there has just threatened me officer," she said, turning to point at the woman who had threatened her, but both #3 and #7 had disappeared, wandering off back into Soho and their car and a return to pass on feedback to Kang at Whitchitley Hall.

"Madam, there is no one there," replied the policeman who was called Officer Thompson, believing the woman was a little senile or worse still – she'd already been drinking at this time of the day. Looking around he was unsure of who she was accusing, the only person in that direction was '*Old Whimper*' one of the local tramps, propped up next to the newsagents on the pavement, already swigging cider out of a bottle, partially hidden in a brown paper bag.

Then Officer Thompson walked straight across the road, with the elderly lady following close behind him, mumbling to herself about '*foreigners coming over here and threatening upstanding members of the community.*'

"What's up Old Whimper?"

"Fuck off I'm on a personal stake out," he replied, taking another swig of cider, wiping the sticky dribbles from his face with the back of his hand. Delving into his pocket he pulled out a half-chewed pork pie, picking the hairs and fluff from it, he popped it into his mouth and chewed wildly with his mouth wide open, crumbs falling off his chin and onto his jumper.

"There's no need for that attitude, you don't want another trip down to the cells again, do you?"

Old Whimper shrugged his shoulders and coughed bits of pork pie and cider globules into the cold Soho air. "I'm just watching what's happening around here, ever since last night," he belched, the smell of his breath reaching both Thompson and the woman over his shoulder and making them both cough.

"Why? What did you see?" Thompson asked, getting out his crumpled notebook and wetting the end of his pencil with his tongue, in preparation for taking notes.

"Well, I couldn't believe my eyes and I've seen a lot of strange things over the years in Soho, from naked women running in the streets to a black elephant rampaging into the Duke of Argyll – I've seen it all, you believe me, don't you?" He queried, his crusty eyebrows raising as he began to recall his thoughts.

Officer Thompson and the elderly '*churchgoer*' looked at each other, both raising their brows in unison as well, as they prepared to listen to the tall tale that was about to be recounted by a man who was obviously imagining or hallucinating about the events of the previous evening.

"Yes, we believe you; what can you tell us then?"

After another gulp of cider and another obligatory wipe of his lips, Old Whimper began to recall what he had seen overnight in the street in Soho.

"Well, I was sat in the doorway, it was late, I'm not sure exactly what time it was but it was dark, and I was dozing in and out of sleep. I'd been in the Duke of Argyll for a few hours where a couple of holidaymakers – Tyrone and Elisa from Buffalo, New York – had taken pity on me, though I didn't need their pity, but what I was happy to take was their near endless supply of drinks that they plied me with," began the tramp as he pulled his hat off and rubbed at what was left of the hair on his head.

"They were really interested in telling me and relishing in the fact, that Buffalo was the second largest city in the state and that they had both lived there all their lives. They went on to tell me that they had met at an Eagles concert in 1971, before the band had become the stars that they were gradually becoming now. But what they were more interested in was me telling them about the porn industry and what happens in Soho, after hours."

Thompson continued to do what policemen did, to make notes, the 'churchgoer' continued to listen in, standing behind him with a handkerchief up to her nose and mouth, trying to mask the smell that was emanating from Old Whimper, like an 'aftershave of the streets'.

Clearing his throat and then taking another swig of the cider, Old Whimper continued with his story of the previous evening.

"They wanted to know everything that I knew about the strip clubs, the seedy cinemas, and the brightly lit sex shops, with their neon signs and multi-coloured strip blind doorways.

I tried to tell them as much as I could, but the more, I told them, the more drinks they gave me, to keep my storytelling lubricated and entertainingly flowing. It eventually got to closing time and they said their farewells and we were all asked to leave. I walked up the road to the junction with Wardour Street and sat down behind a couple of huge industrial street bin. Old Man Johnson was already asleep there and so I made myself comfortable and started to bed down for the night."

Old Whimper rubbed at his chin like he was being bitten by something and then he carried on.

"Just as I was starting to drift off, a black car appeared and two women, both in leather – just like those two girls that were here earlier, the ones you were speaking to, but not them – got out and walked towards the Golden Palace, walking around it, beside it, trying to look in the windows - it almost looked like they were casing the joint; but why would two women be trying to break in to a strip-club that was still open? Then people came out the front door - 'punters' - probably the only ones that were in there, it was a very quiet night in Soho, well it is February and too cold to be out really. The women in black continued to walk around the building, eventually disappearing around the back and into the lane behind the club – I could see all this perfectly from where I was sitting, through the small gap between the two bins.

The tramp then moved, like only tramps do, from left to right, lifting alternate cheeks from off the cold pavement and then back down again.

"It gets cold sitting here on the pavement, even my coat makes little difference."

"I'm sure it doesn't! Ever thought about staying in a hostel?" asked Thompson, the woman nodding behind him.

"No, it's not for me, too much socialising and a high chance of arguments or fights," he replied, belching a 'cidery' burp in the face of his audience, the woman shaking her head in shame; '*manners maketh the man*,' she thought to herself.

"Where was I? Oh yes, sat behind the bins!!! Well, I was tired, it had been a long night and talking constantly to Tyrone and Elisa, for what seemed like hours had truly taken it out of me – I should be paid by the London Council for providing a service like this, I mean people get paid much more for doing a lot less.

Anyway, I was trying to get comfortable and have a little bit of shut eye and was just getting settled, when I saw those two women – the ones all in leather – come out of the front doors of the venue and then they seemed to be locking the front doors. '*Odd*' I thought to myself, how on earth did they have the keys to the place? Made fuck all sense to me."

The 'churchgoer' put her hands over her ears; she was not made to hear such blasphemous language.

Realising what he had said, Old Whimper put his hands up to his mouth and apologised profusely to the old lady, embarrassed that he had upset her - he might have been tatty, but he did have manners - and then carried on.

"Well, they left in a black car, one of those like in that film, whatever it was and then I fell asleep. Must have been an hour later and I was woken up by what sounded like World War III taking off and the building opposite us – the Golden Palace – had erupted into a huge ball of flame and the windows all shattered, spraying shards of glass down on Black Jake, Bobby Martyns and Bozo – all other 'men of the street' – and I jumped up and helped Old Man Johnson up as well and we both ran to their aid. They were covered in blood from a thousand tiny cuts or so it seemed, but they were just as much in shock as we were at what had happened just across the road."

"Okay sir, but is that all you saw, nothing else but these two black leather clad women?" asked Thompson, slowly starting to put away his notebook in his inside pocket.

"No, this is where it all gets a little confusing," he said scratching at his arm like the fleas were extra hungry today. "The flames raged, the fire engines and the police arrived, they took care of a woman who turned up on the scene – Melanie she's called, Melanie Moist – and then one of the firemen left eventually with her in his car."

"We know all of this already," replied Thompson, buttoning up his jacket, deciding that no further notes were going to be needed, but then Old Whimper carried on.

"When everyone had left, except for a couple police officers at each side of the now fenced off smoking ruins, I saw them."

Thompson and the woman leant in, waiting with bated breath to hear what this revelation was going to be, Thompson taking his notebook and pencil back out of his jacket, ready to finish his note taking.

"I was able to see them just like you and me now."

"Who? Who did you see?" probed Thompson, sweat now breaking out on his forehead and gradually beginning to drift and dribble down toward his eyebrows.

"Well, I saw all the people who worked in the club. They came out through the front door, they didn't open it – they came right through it, one after the other, twelve of them. There was Chumpy, Katerina, Ophelia, and the other girls who I don't really know their names and all the door staff, Nat, and Everard and even Biffo, all walking out of the club in a line, almost like they were marching - going somewhere with a clear sense of purpose."

Thompson was worried now and looking around over his

shoulder, jumped, as the old woman was so close to him that he could smell her Extra Strong Mints and hairspray – him jumping, made her jump too.

"Then, they all walked through the fence, they seemed to shimmer as they all passed through it and then within seconds they faded away as they headed – very quickly – down Wardour Street in the direction that the fireman had gone with Melanie, I was so shook up I had to start drinking my secret stash of cider that I had hidden in the bin outside the newsagents."

"Stuff and nonsense," said the old woman as she felt like she was getting nowhere with her complaint against the now long-gone woman and nodding her head to the policeman, she stormed off towards Piccadilly tube station and some normality.

Thompson stood back from Old Whimper, making a breathable space between them like he had the plague and said, "Okay sir, I'll keep hold of those notes and write them up for a report later."

"Scared the shit out of me. I think I've seen the spirits of the dead, the walking dead, I don't want to see them ever again, it'll turn me drink…"

Thompson raised his eyebrows.

"It'll turn me to more drink?" he replied, leaning back against the wall, his eyes drooping as he fell asleep, it had been a long day and it was already past lunchtime.

Thompson walked slowly back towards the fence that he was supposed to be guarding, checking the quality of the barrier, constantly glancing around, as if he were looking for the ghostly spirits that the old tramp had mentioned.

Walking to the other side of the barrier, he walked up to the other policeman, Officer Campbell and nodded a quick hello.

"I've had a real spooky encounter just then. That guy across the road, the old tramp, told me that he saw two women locking up the building and then the explosion happened a little later. But this is the most terrifying scary bit, he said that in the morning he saw twelve ghostly figures – these were perfect visions of the people who had died in the fire - leave the building and walk off in the direction of Shaftsbury Avenue. Jesus, I felt scared as he told us."

"Who was it that told you?" asked Campbell, picking at his teeth with a small toothpick.

"Old Whimper, the alcoholic."

Campbell looked at him and replied.

"You want spooky? Old Whimper died last week of hypothermia, drank himself to death on the street on that really cold night, last Thursday."

With that Thompson looked across the road and there was no one there. No one was sat outside the newsagents, that area of the street was completely empty.

Chapter 8: 'Make It With You'

Monster Mag

Released first in 1973 and costing only 15p, 'Monster Mag' was the horror poster magazine of choice for fans of gore, classic horror, and new releases all over the UK. If you were young and able to find a newsagent's that would sell you it, then you were in for a bloodthirsty treat. Lasting for a short run of 14 issues in 1973, but then was ended, with it revived for a short period of time and 3 issues in 1976. Featuring the best of classic horror – Hammer, Amicus, Tyburn etc – and features on newer released films, the magazine was in full colour and folded out into a massive poster (24" x 36"), all the first volume of issues featured one huge poster, the second volume included some half sized double posters. Reprints of these issues are now available via the Monster Mag Facebook page.

******

"They seem to think that it's a bitter rivalry between the sex industry businesses in Soho – '*Porno Turf War*' was how the policeman at the scene of the clubs ruins described it and that was what he seemed to believe," recounted #1 to Kang, as he was practicing his topiary on a tiny tree on the table in the conservatory - performing the ancient Chinese art of Shumu Penjing – from which the other art of Bonsai developed. #1 had been fed back all the information by #3 and #7 on their return to Whitchitley Hall, just this afternoon.

"Good news then, your team has done me well. But what of the 'Moist woman'?" Kang asked as he carefully snipped away at the outer extremities of the tiny tree, being careful not to trim the branches back too far. He was planning on taking up Shuihan Penjing with his next specimen where the art was to create a landscape using water and rocks, maybe even add some tiny figures too, it was very relaxing for him, especially when he had a lot on his mind, which with his plans was most of the time.

"The Moist woman was seen leaving the scene with a fireman, he took her to his house as she had nowhere to go, now that the Golden Palace is no more," she replied, as she watched Kang snipping away with a tiny, but affective, pair of stainless-steel scissors, that would have looked more appropriate for an experienced manicurist to use.

"Then your next job is to find her and get rid of her. A little accident and the only missing cog in this sex industry machine will be gone and we can then plan what we do next in Soho. You have my full support in all your actions."

With her instructions fully understood, #1 left the room and headed back to her group's quarters, ready to plan and utilize the skills that they had, to try and finish off the final member of the strip club's staff.

Back in his room Kang took a phone call, putting his scissors down next to his miniature tree, when he realised who was calling.

"Yes father, it's all in hand. My security team is looking into finding the final woman who was not in the building at the time of the explosion, the conclusion of this won't be long, and you have my word on that."

Kang nodded to the words that were being fed into his ear from his father on Lamma Island, nearly 6,000 miles away - that was the magic of telecommunications now in the 1970's, and both Kang Senior and Junior believed greatly in the fact that all the areas of the world had been brought much closer together and so work could easily be demanded from China and carried out in London. Life was truly becoming 'modern'.

"Yes father, I will keep you up to date with what is happening, and I'll ring you again at the same time in a few days, I have complete faith in my team successfully eliminating the woman that is still out there."

More nodding ensued from Kang as he listened once more to his father's deep baritone voice, booming down the line from China.

"Her name is Moist, Melanie Moist," he said hanging up.

Chapter 9: 'Lido Shuffle'

Pacers, Spangles, and the Dentist

Sweets in the '70s were the dentist's best friend. Nothing kept the dental practitioners in work more so than the sweets that were available for children to spend their pocket money on. Pacers (mint chews) were like Opal Fruits (Starburst) in their consistency and had the added ability to attach themselves to fillings and remove bits or all of them in one fell swoop. Spangles were like solid candy, but when you bit into them shards would splinter off, leaving you with a mouth full of candied glasslike splinters – they were also excellent for cracking and chipping teeth.

******

"Chumpy, I'm not feeling so well, I think I'm hallucinating."

Resting on the bed, with the covers still wrapped around her, Melanie peaked out over the bed clothes at the twelve people crowded into the small room all looking at her, all jostling for space and giving her knowing nods and winks. They seemed to be there, '*but weren't they all dead from the fire?*' Melanie thought to herself.

"Melanie, we need your help," replied Chumpy Tuppence, a look of worry and confusion on her glowing ethereal face.

"But you're all... Dead?"

"We may be all dead but look what they've done to my bloody club!!!" announced Biffo McGuire waving his arms around in the air, his hands floating through the other bodies as he gesticulated. He was clearly very angry at the situation in Soho, but not completely aware of his own personal situation, which was also just as permanent and final. "I'm not sure if I can handle this?" said Melanie, smiling at the entities hovering around her bed.

"You have to be able to handle this, as we desperately need your help," began Chumpy. "We're all stuck in this place, some kind of unearthly netherworld, somewhere between the living and the dead. None of us are at peace and this G-string is what I must wear from now until the end of eternity," she continued, scratching at her behind through her bright red velvet hot pants.

"I'm not happy either, I was due to go to my sister's birthday party tomorrow and I have no chance of that now," said Katerina Ooglestop, tossing her ginger hair around as she slowly tried to come to terms with her current and ongoing situation.

Melanie looked at all the pleading faces, some angry, some sad, they were staring at her and looking for help and a modicum of hope.

"Apparently we're stuck in this nowhere place until someone can help solve our murders and Melanie Moist, you're the only person that we feel we can depend on," chipped in Tuna Tunnel, flapping her arms around as she always did to emphasise a point, amazed that they could now pass through the bodies of her ghostly colleagues with ease.

"How can I help though? I wouldn't even know where to start on something like this?"

"Ah, but that's where we can help you Melanie," chipped in Chumpy, "we don't know exactly who is to blame for destroying the Golden Palace and as I was saying to the others – when we were in the waiting room – we need to get whoever it was to answer for his actions."

"In the waiting room?" Queried Melanie, sitting up, still feeling like she was 'away with the fairies' or drunk on some strong hooch.

Chumpy sat down on the edge of the bed, a very slight indentation occurring as she lowered herself onto the covers.

"The waiting room is where you go when you die. When we arrived there, it was already busy, but within a few hours dozens more people turned up as well. The room was full of people checking in and all the ones that are straightforward go through the doors to the transport section, with tickets to go up there or down below," she motioned with her thumbs, "and anyone who has died in any strange or unplanned situations are left in the waiting room, with only the chance to come back to Earth to sort out what happened or sit in the waiting room forever and ever."

"What do you mean by 'unplanned situations?'" Melanie enquired, this whole situation was becoming more and more interesting, and she was gradually beginning to understand what was happening and becoming a little 'cooler' with the situation.

"Well, that's what they call the suicide cases," Chumpy replied, "there were lots of them just sitting there, I was talking to the actress Bella Darvi and Pete Duel from 'Alias Smith and Jones' – God I loved that TV show, I was so upset when he shot himself, he was a poster on my wall at my parent's house, before I moved into the Golden Palace. Ernest Hemingway was there too, but he had such a massive crowd around him that I didn't get a chance to speak, but I could hear him recanting tales of his adventures and it was taking a lot of people's minds off the situation that they were now in. Some people were still talking to him instead of moving into the transport section, but they were hurried along by the 'movers' – the winged guys who made sure that there was a steady flow out of limbo."

Melanie continued nodding her head, as the story of what happened to the '*living dead*' was getting more and more interesting, and believable, by the minute. But then she shook her head and pinched the flesh on her arm really hard as she shut her eyes tight, trying to see if it was all a dream.

"Ouccchhhhhh!" She shrieked at the pain in her arms as her nails dug into the surface of her flesh, opening her eyes she could see the mark that she'd left and when she looked up, they were all still there.

Looking.

Pleading.

Their faces told the truth, they were still in the room, and they weren't going to be going anywhere until she helped them out, trapped in limbo currently checked into the *'waiting room'* and looking for the ability to leave the waiting area for suicide victims and head onto the transport and off to better, more relaxed, things.

"Okay, I guess I'll have to help you all then?" Melanie began, an overwhelming sense of happiness radiating from her glowing ethereal friends, all smiling faces, and semi-transparent bodies.

"Please can we get on with this as soon as possible? I can't be bothered listening to that dreadful Hemingway rambling on about his Mojito's in Cuba for the umpteenth time since we've been here and it was only last night that we checked in," crooned Nat King Cock, still in character from his tribute act.

Melanie threw her hands up in the air and smiled at the crowd of all her friends.

'How can I not help them? They need me more now than they ever have,' she thought to herself, *'this is probably the scariest thing that I have ever seen, but as they're my friends it seems to make it so much easier???'*

"Right, please tell me what you know, and I will aim to help you get on your way; I'll do the very best I can."

All the 'unlucky 12' smiled at her.

They knew that they would be able to depend on their friend, she was always the one who took control of the girls at the club and organised the nights out and 'adventures', she would help them to leave the 'waiting room' and move on to pastures new and a place without Cuban drinks and authors ranting.

"Melanie, I think that we need to find Memory Lane to tell you everything she knows – and she knows a lot as well," said Chumpy, sitting forward on the bed.

"Memory had gone to a party on a recent night, not far from London and she was on to something or someone and I believe – from what she was telling me – that he was quite a devious and unscrupulous character from what she said…"

Chapter 10: 'Rhinestone Cowboy'

A Bionic Man, Woman and Dog

The 1970's were full of amazing, thought provoking, educational entertainment and then there were series like this as well!

'The Six Million Dollar Man' was based around the character Steve Austin played by Lee Majors, who went into space on a NASA mission, had an accident and was rebuilt with 'bionic' implants and body parts. With a repaired right arm, both legs and a telescopic vision left eye, Steve went to work for a top-secret agency OSI (Office of Scientific Intelligence) and fought crime all over the USA – even at one time in '76 encountering and fighting Bigfoot.

"We can rebuild him; we have the technology" was the catchphrase which sold the show and as it proved a hit from the start the inevitable was bound to happen – a spin off with Lindsay Wagner as 'The Bionic Woman. Wagner played Jamie Sommers a tennis star who had a skydiving accident and was again rebuilt by Oscar Goldman and Dr. Rudy Wells – who had previously repaired Steve Austin. She was equipped with a pair of bionic legs and right arm, but unlike Austin, she was given a bionic ear, which gave her the ability to eavesdrop on criminals from a distance.

There were plans for another spin off series 'the Bionic Dog' but that only ended up as a two-part episode in Season 3 of 'The Bionic Woman' with a dog called Max who was given a bionic jaw and four bionic legs.

******

Well, I guess I'll give you the benefit of the doubt then?" sighed Nancy as she rolled to her right in the bed, coming face to face with Byron, who'd sneaked back in, leaving the sofa downstairs behind.

It was just after 1pm and the rain outside was crashing and splashing against the window and wind was blowing the tree around, the branches tapping on the glass panes like spindly fingers, poking and prodding and pointing at the talking lovers in the warmth of their bed.

"I'm sorry I upset you Nancy, I know that we haven't been having the best of times, with your hours and combined with our shifts always seeming to clash, it hasn't been good, but I still want our relationship to last, I still love you, you know!"

"Then prove it," she said pulling off her top and rolling closer to Byron.

As their skin touched each other that old 'electricity' began to ramp up and as they tore off each other's final items of clothing, it was like 'old times', when they were first together and before the arguing had begun.

Their arguments of late had almost started them hating each other, bordering on loathing each other's touch on their skin.

But not tonight...

Maybe it was the thought that he had been so truthful and honest about the naked stripper in the spare room or the fact that she now believed him and felt that she trusted him totally once more, but there seemed to be a new energy to their lovemaking and as they carried on the passion increased ten-fold, it was like old times, before the heated and furious arguments and nights of not talking to each other.

As he rolled on top of her and thrust away like a steam train taking the mail to the next town, Byron looked up at the wall and could've sworn that he saw something, perhaps a pair of eyes looking at him and Nancy, staring at their most intimate of moments.

He blinked his eyes and just as he did a face, then a full head and a hand appeared through the wall. The face winked at him, and the hand gave him the thumbs up and then slowly Everard Koch, his hair greased down and his pencil moustache waxed to points, faded back into the wall, and disappeared.

"What the fuck!!!" Shouted Byron, his pounding rhythm affected, and his motion turned into chaos, the moment was gone and as he lost his erection, Nancy asked him what was wrong.

"Are you okay? What's the matter?"

Byron climbed back off of Nancy and banged the flat of his palm on the wall, checking to see if there was something wrong with it, but it was a solid piece of internal wall, and the only reaction was a loud slap when his skin hit the surface of the wallpaper.

"Sorry, I thought I saw something on the wall," replied a clearly shaken Byron, looking totally baffled as to what he'd just witnessed.

"Oh god, I hope we don't have cockroaches again," exclaimed Nancy as she put an arm around Byron's shoulder, trying to coax him back into the bed, but the moment had passed, and they would have to pick up where they were later that evening as neither of them were working.

"No, it wasn't bugs, it most definitely wasn't bugs!"

"So, what do you think you saw honey?" asked Nancy, using her best nursing skills and sensing that Byron was a little shaken by the 'something' that he'd seen.

Shaking his head once more, as if to get rid of any visions that were still floating around in there, Byron sat up and moved along the bed to the wall, tapping at it as he tried to see if there was some kind of panel or opening that he'd never spotted before – which seemed like a totally ridiculous idea when he thought it over again.

"I thought that I saw a face and a hand coming out of the wall…" Nancy looked at him quizzically. Was he drunk or had he not had enough sleep and was just hallucinating? From her years of nursing experience, she was aware of this happening to lots of people over the years, worse if they were driving or operating machinery, like the guy that had been working at the Ford car factory in Dagenham one evening when she had been on shift.

******

It had been ten years ago when she had started work at Rush Green Hospital near Romford, where she'd worked until she moved to her current job at Old Church Hospital. There had been reports of a major accident coming in from the Ford car plant, as they were the nearest hospital and they didn't think that the employee would be able to make it any further, due to massive blood loss.

Nancy had been one of the nurses on duty that night and was told by the matron that she would need to go down to the emergency check-in to aid the paramedics as they were bringing in a man who had been involved in an accident on the production line at the car factory in Dagenham, just down the road.

With flashing lights and sirens blaring, the ambulance could be heard in the distance and as it came through the gates and pulled up at the side of the hospital, Nancy and the other nurses and a night shift junior doctor, ran to help. The ambulance driver climbed out of the front of the vehicle and his colleague who was in the back flung open the door and moved the trolley to the edge of the doorway. The driver came around to the back of the ambulance and both team members pulled the man on trolley out into the doorway of the hospital.

Nancy had never in all her days of nursing, seen so much blood.

The man, from the look of it was in his mid to late 50's. He was probably a little overweight and had long hair or to say it correctly, he had once had a full head of long hair.

Half of the side of the man head was gone and with it half his hair. "Get him in quickly," shouted a member of the ambulance crew, "he's lost a lot of blood already. I've managed to stem the flow, but he's in a very bad way.

With that, he was whisked away, through the doors and right into the emergency department.

Rush Green hospital usually dealt with maternity cases and emergency caesarians, so this was totally different to the usual daily cases, but needs must as he was too ill to make it any further - as they had been told by dispatch, when he was on his way.

"Can you help move him onto a bed," asked an ambulance man, nodding at Nancy and her matron, as they stood next to the bed.

Holding the sheets, they gently rolled the patient onto the bed, more blood splashing on them and dripping on their uniforms as they eased him onto the mattress.

It was only when they pulled back the sheet that he was wrapped in that they saw the full extent of his injuries and it made a little bit of sick come up into Nancy's mouth as she looked down on the disfigured body that was laid out in front of her.

Not only had the man before them been partially scalped, but also all his fingers on his left hand had been severed to the knuckle. Where the fingers had been completely removed, the heat must have cautorised the wounds and instead of a bleeding hand before them, they had what now resembled a crusty, burnt paw, like that of an animal or a singed boxing glove.

There were also burn marks right up the left arm and deep gouges from something hot that must have scorched him whilst he was working on this shift, which would probably be his last due to his manual dexterity now being severely impaired.

The older of the two ambulance paramedics then gave a full detailed report of what had happened and then recounting the series of events since arriving at the scene of the accident.

The victim's name was John Wilson and he had been working on the production line at the Dagenham Ford plant and had gone to the use the 'abrasive wheels' to grind down a metal bracket that he was attempting to attach - by welding - to the engine block of the car that he was working on. The bracket had been very, very slightly miss-cast and so he only had to grind a few millimetres off the left-hand side of the outside edge and that would've been the job done. As he had turned on the grinding wheels, he had apparently blinked a few times, according to someone who was standing nearby and then shut his eyes. Wilson had been out all night, the day before at a party and had not slept at all for over 24hrs. Normally at work he would have worn a hair net or had his hair pulled into a tight ponytail and had a cap on top to hold it all in place, but due to his lack of sleep he'd failed to do either and his hair was hanging loose and that's where he made his momentous mistake.

With his hair hanging loose, he leant forward, with his eyes closed getting nearer and nearer to the speedily revolving stone wheels. One of his work colleagues called to him to watch out and then he opened his eyes again but made the mistake of turning his head and as he did, his hair fell onto one of the spinning wheels.

Rapidly his hair became entangled in the wheel and within a blink of a second his hair was torn from his head, with half his scalp and a large swathe of skin down the side of his face. In all the chaos, he tried to stop the wheel, grabbing at it with his left hand and immediately grinding and slicing away his fingers. His fingers were ground down to the knuckles in a matter of seconds, with bone and flesh spraying out in an arc, as the heat from the spinning wheel stopped the bleeding and burnt his fist, sealing the wound. The bloody remains of his fingers were flung across the shop floor and blood began to pour from his head as he began screaming in shock at the searing pain - eventually fainting when he looked down at what remained of his left fist. His friends had hit the '*power-off*' emergency electricity breaker, to stop the wheels and collected up the shredded remains of his bloodstained fingers, especially as one of the loose digits, was still wearing his scuffed and dented wedding ring.

Lack of sleep causes accidents. Lack of sleep causes hallucinations, sometimes in the most extremes of circumstances.

******

So, it was possible that due to the lack of sleep Byron was hallucinating or dreaming, it couldn't be explained any other way, thought Nancy to herself, as Byron continued to tap and slap the wall as if there was some kind of 'fake panel' in it or like a magician's trapdoor.

"There's nothing there," said Byron, still rapping on the wall with his knuckles, like the Raven in Poe's classic poem.

Nancy sat up and put an arm around her boyfriend's shoulders.

"Darling, I'll go instead and make us some lunch, you have a little sleep here in bed and I'll bring it up for you when it's ready. Do you think Melinda will want anything, I'm sure she's tired and hungry still?"

"Melanie, she's called Melanie," replied Byron, laying back down in the bed, his eyes darting rapidly from side to side, looking for anything strange that was happening in the bedroom.

"Melinda, Melanie – whatever!!! I'll go and see if she wants anything."

With that Nancy left the room, with Byron lying on the bed, his neck stretched backwards looking at the wall and repeatedly shaking his head, completely confused as to what he'd seen or what he'd possibly seen.

As Nancy shut the door and crossed the landing, she could hear voices coming from the spare bedroom.

"*I can't believe it, she's brought a bloody punter into our house - she is a fucking prostitute,*" thought Nancy to herself as she crept across the twenty feet to the bedroom, the floorboards creaking as she did. Trying to walk slower, gently raising her left foot and then pushing down with her toes as she lifted her right foot, the voices in the room continued, not easing up at all.

"There's more than two voices in there," she whispered to no one in general, "she is using our house as a flippin' knocking shop," she continued as she neared the door.

Nancy knocked on the door and all the voices inside went silent.

"Come in," the voice replied, and Nancy opened the door to find Melanie sat on her own on the bed, wrapped in the covers and no one else in the room.

"Did I hear voices a moment ago? I could've sworn I heard you talking to some people in here?"

Melanie smiled, "nope, only little old me," she replied smiling, looking both nervous and happy at the same time.

"Are you sure? I thought I heard people talking to you. You haven't invited 'friends' over to stay, have you?" asked Nancy, looking around the room, but seeing no one and as there were no wardrobes in there, just an open clothes rail, there was nowhere that anyone could have hidden, especially at such short notice as she opened the door.

Blushing, Melanie bit at her lip as she attempted to provide an answer that didn't sound made up or false.

"I was just talking to myself about what I was going to do now that I have nowhere to live and answering in the voices of my friends?" she said, her reply sounding like a query at the end and almost questioning her own answer and her sanity.

Nancy looked at Melanie and thought to herself that the poor girl had, had a very bad night and so it was probably the full string of events, that was playing on her mind, and she needed, just like Byron, to get plenty more rest; after a few more hours sleep, her 'house guest' would be feeling much better, she was sure.

"Do you want anything to eat later?" asked Nancy, taking pity on Melanie, "I can come back in an hour or so, if that's okay?"

Melanie nodded in reply - as Nancy turned and left the room - blushing a little as she really didn't know what to say or how she was going to cope with these 'visitations.

It was going to take a lot of getting used to.

Chapter 11: 'Kid Charlemagne'

'Girrrl Power'

The 1970's were a time of great TV shows and there were plenty of them, but none showed 'Girl Power' like 'Charlie's Angels'. A crack team of Police Academy graduates – Sabrina Duncan, Jill Munroe, and Kelly Garrett – were given menial jobs instead of important police work, parking meter maid, office worker and a crossing guard. Leaving the police force, all three of them went to work for 'Charlie' of the Charles Townsend Agency – all working together as PI's. The Angels were played by Kate Jackson (Sabrina), Farrah Fawcett (Jill) and Jaclyn Smith (Kelly) with their NEVER SEEN boss played by John Forsythe of 'Dynasty' fame, but by voice only and never seen in the programme. Their direct line of contact with cases and Charlie was John Bosley played by David Doyle. As the series progressed, Jill was replaced by Cheryl Ladd who played her sister Kris Munroe, Sabrina was replaced by Shelley Hack as Tiffany Wells and then she finally left and was replaced by Tanya Roberts as Julie Rogers – so Kelly was the only Angel to stay the course for the whole five seasons of the series and Bosley was also in every one of the 115 action packed episodes, to help her.

******

The basement at Whitchitley Hall was a vast sprawling underground concrete bunker - no windows, no natural light and was currently used as a training ground for M.D.S.

The south end was a sealed off gun practice site, a full shooting range with targets and the use of a wide variety of handheld weapons, from semi-automatic pistols and vintage guns to rifles and machine guns.

#3 was currently blindfolded, standing at a workbench just outside the range and with no use of sight at all, was dismantling and reassembling her Kalashnikov AK-47, with the speed of someone with 20/20 vision.

The Avtomat Kalashnikova or AK, was #3's weapon of choice and her preferred tool for any and pretty much every situation. The weapon had a gas operated rotating bolt and could fire 600 rounds a minute or in semi-automatic mode 40 rounds a minute or could easily fire off short bursts of 100 rounds a minute and you could pretty much destroy your enemy or a small army in a minute or less at the best of times.

Clicking the final parts into place she slammed her rifle down on the bench in front of her, removing her blindfold to see if she had finally won a victory over her colleague.

#7 had clicked the stopwatch as the rifle was smashed down on the wooden surface and prepared to tell #3 the result.

"That's five seconds faster than your previous best," said #7, picking at her nails with one of her sharpest blades, the knife glinting and sparkling from the overhead lighting.

"I must be faster, my father always told me that I should be able to beat my brother as I was much more dexterous than him, but my brother is still slightly quicker, I must improve. Time me again."

With that she put her blindfold back on again and when #7 told her to begin, her nimble fingers went to work on the weapon once more, flashing across the well-oiled tool, like greased lightning.

At the other end of the basement was a full-sized gym and #4 was practising her karate moves on a Wing-Chun dummy – her 'wooden man post' - made of solid wood and designed for people to use arm and leg work and develop their fighting skills.

Kick after well-honed kick, chop after deadly chop, slap after forceful slap, #4 laid into the piece of solid wood exercise equipment like her life depended on it, taking no prisoners as she continued to pummel and batter the unit until her hands and feet had turned pink and sore.

#1 stood to the side of the gym area watching #4 practising.

"Harder, faster," she called, egging her comrade on, as #4 didn't let up, although she had been going in this current bout for over ten minutes.

"We take no prisoners," shouted #1, making her team member speed up and continue faster until with one almighty chop, she broke one of the protruding wooden arms off, a spray of splinters showering over the practice mats.

#4 bowed to her dummy and turned to face #1.

"I think we may need to get another Wing-Chun; I appear to have made this one slightly disabled."

Bringing her hands together and clapping heartily, #1 nodded her head in agreement.

"A new arm will be procured for your next practice session, your Wing-Chun will be like new once more."

#4 laughed, bowing to #1 as she left the gym area and headed to the changing rooms for a shower and to get dressed back into her work clothes.

The elite squad were extremely conscientious and being at the peak of their physical and mental fitness was paramount to all of them. Being at the topmost of their abilities meant that they were a force to be reckoned with and all their skills combined meant that they were virtually invincible, which is how they wanted to be thought of especially by their employer Sébastien Kang.

Kang would occasionally come down to the basement to take in a training session, watching from the wings as they fought, shot, and threw knives at targets. He was also very interested in the bomb and trap making skills of #2 and the chemist abilities of #6 as she made up her scientific cocktails of poisons, truth serums and chemical compounds which would render their victims with the inability of movement, totally stopping them in their tracks and ending any action or headway, making them appear dead or even 'undead', as the case would usually seem.

Then - as if on cue – the doorway to the basement opened and Kang slowly walked down the stairs, cane in hand as he tapped and limped his way down the wooden steps, ending up in the underground room.

"Where is #1?"

Looking around the floor, Kang tried to locate the leader of the M.D.S. and spotted her at the far end, monitoring the progress of #1 on the rifle range and checking that #7 was timing her dismantling and reassembling skills accurately.

#1 looked up and immediately walked the length of the basement to meet with Kang. The time it took was over 30 seconds; the full length of the basement was that long, and the staircase entryway was directly the opposite end to the practice range. Walking towards Kang, #1 passed the beds for her crew, basic military style single beds, eight in number, with a rudimentary locker and bedside cabinet next to each bed plus a small lamp on top, all with the same blood red flowered lampshades – looking like the only hint at the decade that they were living in and the only 'glam' element of the dormitory area. As she passed the beds and entered the recreational area, she once again remembered what had happened to number eight, just over a year before.

******

#8 had skills unlike any of the others in the M.D.S., she was blessed with a photographic memory plus she had superior observation, investigative and research skills. Bordering a fine line between genius and madwoman, she was more intelligent than #1, her British MENSA score was one of the highest that they had ever recorded since their inception in 1946 - #8's IQ registered at 210, which was only 18 points less than Marilyn vos Savant of St. Louis, Missouri, who was the current Guinness Book of Records holder, with an IQ score of 228 - #1's IQ stood at a much poorer 180, but still made her a genius and she was a natural born leader, ideally fitted to command the M.D.S.

When they had arrived in Felixstowe by boat that night, they had been collected by Kang's security team and taken to their new quarters at Whitchitley Hall and chose their beds in the underground dormitory.

#8 emptied her bags, hanging her clothes up in the locker and sitting down on her bed, which was the one between the beds of #3 and #6.

Ever since they had all met up to get the boat in Murmansk, something had been nagging at #8. She recognised #6, but even her excellent memory couldn't exactly work out where. The fact that they all were only known by numbers didn't help, if she only knew her name, she would be able to pinpoint exactly where she knew her from, how many times she had met her and even why she wasn't exactly trusting of this member of the M.D.S. With just the smallest bit of information like this she was convinced that all the information regarding her colleague would come flooding back and she'd then be able to sleep comfortably in her bed, knowing that she could either trust or needed to be extremely wary of her team member.

That evening, #8 had picked up her towel and her wash bag and had headed to the showers in the basement, just past the recreational area and just before gym.

The showers were in an adjacent room and were very basic, but just what you'd expect in a military style dormitory. There were six showers, each one separated by a cheap heavy-duty shower curtain. The curtains were fairly see through but gave some privacy unless a body was pushed up against them.

On entering the washing area, #8 could hear four of the showers already going and to be friendly, she went into one next to a shower that was being used, so that she could strike up a conversation with one of the other squad members.

"These showers are quite basic, aren't they?"

"It's nothing more than I would have expected for us," replied the woman in the next cubicle, her naked body barely visible through the plastic sheeting.

"I guess you're right, I was just expecting more, when I saw the building upstairs and how lavish that is."

"You guessed wrong," replied the woman once more.

There was nothing friendly about this exchange, thought #8 to herself as she took her clothing off and turned the shower on, the lukewarm water gradually spraying over her toned naked body. As she gently rubbed the soap into her hands to work up a lather, she started to rub at her breasts and her neck, cleaning the dirt and grime of the last 24hrs off her body as she continued to try and strike up a conversation. "Have you worked in this kind of situation before?" she asked, the soap cascading down her stomach and down across her thighs, leaving a trail of bubbles as it drifted past her crotch, heading southwards towards the drain.

"I have many years of experience, it's what I do," came the reply from the woman, as abrupt and snappy as before.

"Okay…"

Then just as #8 had replied, the woman in the next cubicle bent over to pick up her dropped soap bar and her bottom, bare and pert, pressed against the plastic sheeting and it was then that she noticed the tattoo on the woman's left buttock, pushed against the sheeting the tattoo was clear and quite large and from what it said, she knew that it meant trouble.

Not knowing who was in the shower, #8 tried to squint at the person who was in there, but it was no use, she had moved back from the curtain again and so was just a blurry outline.

Then the lighting went.

The room was suddenly filled with commotion as several of the squad shouted and moaned about the power cut, especially as the water began to rapidly cool. Less than a minute later, the lighting returned, and the warmth of the water increased once again.

Then #8 realised that the woman in the next shower had gone and left the room, but so had two of the others, so she was confused still as to who had the 'tattoo'.

As she wrapped herself in a towel and picked up all her clothes, she left her cubicle and went to exit the shower room, but as she did #2 came out of the shower opposite, which eliminated her from being the tattooed woman.

Walking quickly back to the dormitory area she looked around to see who was still getting dressed and who had wet hair.

#1 was standing talking to #7, neither having wet hair, so obviously neither had just left the shower area. #5 was lying on her bed reading a book, looking comfortable; she'd obviously been there for quite a while.

Which left the others.

As she looked around the beds, she could see that #3 and #4 were both vigorously rubbing at their hair with standard issued towels and as she turned to the squad member next to her, she saw that #6 had a towel on her head as well.

The 'tattooed member' was either #3, #4 or #6 and it was her job to find out and inform #1 of what she had found uncovered.

******

A few days later, still unable to ascertain who the tattooed member of her team was, #8 finally went to see #1 to fully explain the situation and to show her concerns about a possible danger in the crew and a member who was possibly unreliable or a loose cannon.

#8 found her team leader out in the grounds, having a bit of personal time, walking around in the sun, and thinking about her week ahead.

"Hi, I have something that's been on my mind since we arrived here from the boat and it's very concerning," she said as she walked up beside #1. "I can't keep it to myself any longer, it's a fucking worry."

"This is the first time I've had a chance to be on my own."

"Sorry."

#1 looked at #8 and shook her head.

"Go on then, tell me what's on your mind?"

Walking over to a carved stone bench, next to an eight foot rose bush, they both sat down and looked at each other. Although they were now all part of the same team, none of the eight really knew each other very well, just through brief chats and weapons practice, so this was as close as the two members had ever got to each other, and it was difficult for #8 to be completely open with her at the start.

"I feel that we have a problem on the team," she began, trying to explain the situation to her leader the best she could.

"Go on."

Clearing her throat, #8 began to tell #1 what all she knew.

"Going back to the night we arrived from in Felixstowe from Murmansk, we were all new colleagues. None of us really knew each other, I did recognise a couple faces, only because some of our squad had lived in the same area on the Kola Peninsula, but no one that I was able to recognise by name.

When we arrived at Whitchitley we were quickly shown to our basement dormitory, and I took a shower – as did several of the other girls. It was in the showers where I discovered that one of the other bathers had a tattoo on their naked body, large enough for me to read when she was leant against the shower curtain."

#1 looked at her, intrigued as to which way the conversation was heading, leaning back on the stone bench, and staring deep into #8's eyes as she said –

"That tattoo was 1488."

The leader of the M.D.S. sat back, she had heard of this before, but wasn't fully aware of the implications of a member of her team having this tattoo, she nodded to #8 to continue with her revelations and #8 continued, with her photographic memory working overtime on the facts that she had gleaned about the tattoo's meaning and all the information that it represented.

"1488 is a white supremacist tattoo, worn by people who follow Nazi idealisms and for that I feel that this person is possibly dangerous to us and a person that might not be totally trusted in certain situations," she explained, waiting for some feedback from her leader.

#1 sat forward and asked, "What does 1488 actually mean though?"

"I've investigated this, and it isn't good.

1488 is a new code used by Nazi's in the USA. A guy named David Lane has started using it as a cipher to identify other Nazi sympathisers.

The 'Fourteen' represents the fourteen-word phrase that has started to be used by Lane –

'We must secure the existence of our people and a future for White Children'.

The '88' represents the 8th letter of the alphabet - the letter 'H' - the number signifying the phrase 'Heil Hitler'. I don't feel that this person should be part of our group, they are possibly a bad omen for any of our projects and contentious race issues, especially whilst working here for Mr. Kang."

"Very interesting, I'm so glad that you have brought this to my attention, you are an exceptional member of the squad and have already proved yourself to be extremely dependable and reliable. Thank you for all your help, you're dismissed."

With that #1 stood up and left #8 sat on the bench with her thoughts, as she walked back towards the basement entrance, just as it began to rain, sheets of silvery liquid sunshine beating down on the all the areas of the gardens, turning the grass muddy and making #8 run and shelter in the concrete gazebo in the garden area.

The gazebo was located outside the entrance to the large maze, which was made of ten-foot high bushes and covered a vast area – people had been known to get lost in there and take over four hours to find their way out, it was at one of Kang's summer soirees that some party guests had got lost in there and had to be pinpointed by the high security cameras and retrieved by the houses security staff.

As #8 stood watching the rain pouring down in a torrential shower, #1 went into the dormitory area and made a beeline for #3, who was sat on her bed. As there was no one else in the sleeping area she struck up a hushed conversation with her colleague.

"Your secrets out," she said to her, a look of confusion fleetingly drifting across the face of #3, she playing ignorant to her 'secret' that had possibly been exposed.

"What do you mean?" replied #3, making herself sound confused, but knowing full well what her squad leader was referring to.

This could be it; she might have to go back to Russia and a lack of work, lack of money and a total lack of food.

"Have you got a tattoo?"

"What do you mean, why?" replied #3.

'The game's up, she's going to be shipping me out and I'll be going back to Murmansk, I'll have to find another job and it'll be hell on Earth...' she thought to herself as she stood up, eye to eye with her leader.

"No, lay on the bed and drop your trousers and that's an order."

Sitting back down on the bed – just as she'd been told - #3's fingers slowly began to unbutton herself; she unhurriedly dragged the zip downwards and finally squeezed herself out of the leather trousers. Looking at the ceiling, staring wide-eyed, as she tried to ignore the delving and moving eyes and fingers of her squad leader.

#1 moved her hands deliberately over #3's lower half, searching every cleft and dimple for the tattoo that she couldn't find, her fingers slipping in and out of all her 'areas'.

"Turn over, I want to check everywhere."

With that, she turned over and her tattoo was revealed. 1488, clearly imprinted onto her left buttock in black ink, standing out where no one else could see it or had seen it, but her squad leader and #8.

"Nice tattoo, it matches mine…"

The semi naked squad member on the bed flipped over, her jaw hanging loose as she watched #1 slowly dropping her trousers to reveal a neatly trimmed bush and a smaller 1488 tattooed just above her pubis. "Girls like us need to stick together," said #1 smiling at her new partner in crime and confidant, "we need to talk about #8, she could become a big problem if we don't nip this situation in the bud."

Three days later, at supper time in the mess hall, it was announced that #8 had left the squad and was currently on her way back to be embraced in the arms of Mother Russia on a top-secret mission, which had been authorised by #1 and so she wouldn't be seen again as she would from now on be based out of Moscow.

It was the same evening that the maze was fenced off and a very bold '*no entry*' sign was put up in front of it.

******

#1 stood in front of Kang, it must've been important for him come down to the basement; they very rarely had the honour of their employer going out of his way to talk to them in their quarters.

"We need to find this woman, this Moist woman," said Kang, beads of sweat still on his forehead from his workout in his own personal gym a few moments before.

"I have been thinking about her and she must be the only remaining piece of the jigsaw that we need to remove. We've taken care of the straight edges in the form of the building and the many strange, shaped pieces, which were the staff and the strippers, we just have the one, odd, shaped stripper that has so far eluded me and eluded your supposedly 'crack unit', leaving a gaping hole in a Soho shaped puzzle. You need to prove to me that your unit is still incredibly reliable and that I am getting full value for money."

Kang looked at #1 and she stared back at him, still showing an air of total confidence in her teams' abilities.

"Bring me the head of Melanie Moist."

Chapter 12: 'Hold the Line'

Dirty Harry

In the 1970's there was a new kind of cop on the block. One that lived by his own rules, breaking, and bending the police code for the San Francisco Police Department and at times taking the law into his own hands and working outside the parameters of the forces code of conduct. This cop was Harry Callaghan or 'Dirty Harry' as he was known by.

Clint Eastwood starred in a series of worldwide Box Office smashes, making gritty cop movies, where sometimes the police weren't as righteous and law abiding as they should be.

Three Dirty Harry films were released in the 1970's which were:

'Dirty Harry' 1971, 'Magnum Force' 1973 and 'The Enforcer' in 1976 and giving Clint a catch phrase from the first film in –

"You've got to ask yourself a question: "Do I feel lucky?" Well, do ya, punk?"

******

Melanie Moist moved down the staircase - at the home of Byron and Nancy - like a cat made of honey. She slithered down the flight of steps like a 'slinky toy' as her feline wiles made her look the '*purrfect*' partner as Byron watched her descend over the carpeted stairs like a goddess; if Byron had been single, he would have made a move on her, though the way that the last few months had been with Nancy, he was surprised that they were still a bona fide couple.

The previous few hours with Nancy had been like the old days though and she seemed very happy now, in the kitchen with the radio blaring, singing along at the top of her lungs to '*Brand New Key*' by another Melanie. Where she wasn't sure of some of the lyrics, she '*la la la'd*' making her own harmonies to fit in with the missing words, like some kind of musical jigsaw, with her mind imagining the musical picture on the cover and filling in the gaps.

"Afternoon!!! Do you want something to eat?" asked Nancy, looking over shoulder as Melanie – the singer, not the stripper - came to an end and the music changed to Al Green and his top ten hit 'Let's Stay Together'.

"I love this song! The amount of times I've peeled off my G-string to this in the last few weeks is nobody's business," Melanie blurted out pulling her loaned dressing gown across her magnificent breasts, forgetting that she wasn't in the staff room with some of her stripper friends and club colleagues; though she assumed that they were actually still around in the bedroom upstairs, squeezed in between the bed and the window in limbo, waiting for their ticket out of there and onward to a much better final resting place.

"It's certainly a great song," replied Byron, Nancy looking daggers at him from the sink as she washed the final plates and cups from the day before that had been piled up on the draining board, which was also still covered in the remainders of the Vesta Curry that Byron had picked up on the way home from work.

"Byron, help me with the dishes, whilst I cook something up for our guest."

Melanie smiled, taking a seat at the kitchen table, and looking at the Daily Mirror, which had been delivered as they'd all tried to catch up on their sleep.

"I see we're still rubbish at the Winter Olympics in Japan," Melanie said out loud as she flicked through the pages, from the sport at the back, heading towards the news at the front. "We still haven't won a medal!"

"Not a surprise really, we don't have anywhere for our team to practice – there's never any snow," replied Byron, over the dishes, his back to Melanie, looking out the window as he scrubbed away at the plates.

"I guess…"

As Melanie and Byron chit chatted in the kitchen, Nancy - who seemed to have been forgotten in the ongoing conversation – pottered around in the fridge and the freezer compartment, looking for something that she could 'cobble together' as a meal for their new *'stripper friend'*. Finding some frozen packets, she turned back to Melanie.

"How about some Findus Frozen Crispy Pancakes?" she asked, "and some chips?" she added as she dragged a half-demolished pack of frozen chips out of the tiny freezer compartment in the fridge.

'I'll have to go shopping, when I get the time,' Nancy thought to herself, the fridge only had a piece of processed cheese and four slices of spam and all that was left in the small freezer compartment was half a Swiss Roll.

"That's absolutely fine, I'm famished," Melanie called from the behind the newspaper, sitting up straight, her left boob partially falling out of the dressing gown that was really an ill fit and trying to ease it back in under the clothing before anyone else noticed her faux pas.

"Sorry," she replied as Byron looked over her and smiled, one of the plates slipping from his hands and dropping back into the washing up bowl, with a loud splashing crash.

"Be carefully with those darling, we're down to the last flowery plate of the set, we're going to need to go to Debenhams soon and get a completely new set of crockery. I only just opened the kitchen cupboard the other day and the rectangular dish, that I make the

Cottage Pie's in, slid out and knocked a flowery plate to the floor, smashing it into pieces – I really like them too, took absolutely ages to sweep up all the little bits of china."

'KKKKKKErrracckkkckkkkkckkckck...'

"What the hell was that noise?" asked Byron, looking to Nancy and then to the partially dressed Melanie, who both shook their heads in unison, both having heard the noise, neither having a clue as to what had caused it or where it had come from.

"Give me a second, I'm going to check upstairs."

With that, Byron threw the kitchen towel onto the draining board and dropped the dish that he had been trying to clean, back into the soapy water and left the kitchen at pace.

Climbing the stairs, two steps at a time, Byron was on the landing before anyone else had even left the kitchen and within seconds he was outside his and Nancy's bedroom door. Swinging the door open he checked if anything had fallen off a shelf or the bed, but he observed nothing out of the ordinary or misplaced from its usual position.

Spinning around and going into the bathroom, it was the usual mess of towels, y-fronts, and knickers, all over the floor and the rug was scrunched up on the tiles, as it always seemed to get when someone climbed out of the bath.

Picking up a few bits of the clothes, he put them back in the wash basket and turned around closing the bathroom door as left.

The next room to check was the one Melanie had been staying in and that was the one that seem to be the quietest, there couldn't possibly have been anything happening in there, could there?

Most of the house was warm due to the gas heaters in each room and the hallway, but as he opened the door to the spare bedroom that Melanie had slept in, up until recently, he noticed that the temperature had dropped considerably, so much so, that when he entered the room, he could see his breath, floating around as he exhaled.

A shiver went up Byron's spine as he shook his shoulders together, to try and warm himself up and then he saw it.

As he looked around the room, he was trying to check for anything that had fallen from a shelf or toppled off the bed, after being precariously balanced on there or on the armchair in the corner of the room, there was nothing, but the bed didn't look right.

As he stared at the bed he could see indentations, four sets of them as if four guests were still sitting on top of the candlewick bedspread as he stood there looking. The indentations on the bed appeared to be from four bottoms for people sitting next to each other along the right-hand side of the bed along the edge.

The temperature in the room continued to be ice cold as Byron rubbed his hands together rapidly as he stared at the bottom imprints. Then just as he was staring the indentations gradually began to fade, as if all the 'invisible' people had stood up in unison and moved off the bed and gone to another position, perhaps somewhere else in the bedroom, equally invisible.

Byron had watched many programs over the years about strange phenomena such as poltergeists and spooky situations in old houses, but he had never encountered anything in their home before, at all. Nancy and he had lived a happy life in the house with nothing eerie or anything at all mysterious happening until now, especially after they'd been making love earlier and the hands that had come through the wall, during their most personal of moments.

Byron couldn't believe it.

The more he looked at the bed the more he realised that there was nothing there now, but had there been something there before?

He felt like his mind was playing tricks on him.

He'd seen things like this on TV before when people had been confused - sometimes on drugs, sometimes because of alcohol - but he'd had neither, though he did need a bit more sleep, it had been a long night last night.

There was something going on in his house and the girls were coming up the stairs behind him to find out as well.

"Have you seen anything happening in here?" asked Melanie as she made her way in the door, closely followed by Nancy who was walking just a few short steps behind her on the landing.

"No, there's bugger all here, the only thing I can see is a small ornament on the floor by the window, but that wouldn't have made that big noise. I can't understand it. It's just doing my head in."

And then just as they were all looking at the bed, they noticed a dark shadow go across the window, Byron felt goose pimples rise all over his body as he witnessed the 'shadow-person' slowly move across the room.

But then he realised that this shadow was on the outside and as Byron pulled back the curtains, he realised that the window cleaner was doing his normal rounds outside their house and had just accidentally dropped a full soapy bucket of water – with a mop and wiper - onto the driveway below.

"Sorry," the window cleaner mumbled from outside, "I hope I never woke anyone up?" he mimed through the glazing, his peaked cap holding his hair out of his eyes, his glasses partially steamed up because of the warm and steamy bucket of water, that's contents had slightly poured down the front of his dungarees on their descent to the ground. "Jesus Christ," muttered Byron as he closed the curtains again, turning around to Melanie and Nancy. "I'm sure that's all that the noise was, bloody 'Wally the Window Cleaner' doing his rounds and being clumsy like usual; he's the bloody Essex version of Norman Wisdom." Melanie and Nancy both chuckled, relieved that nothing was happening in the bedroom. Though as Byron and Nancy stood looking around, Melanie saw a different scene totally.

Standing all around the room were her friends, her ghostly deceased friends - visible to her, but apparently completely invisible to her hosts. As they all smiled and nodded and gave their thumbs up and peace signs, Melanie looked at Byron and Nancy and they were both completely oblivious to the spirits, the only effect on them being the lowered temperature in the room.

"Well, I'll be down in a moment, I'll just get changed," she said and with that Nancy ushered Byron out of the door and shut it behind her, Melanie alone, but not alone, in the bedroom once again.

"What the fuck are we going to do now?"

Melanie looked around at all the people shuffling in her room, looking at their feet. It was gradually becoming less unnerving, because although these people were spirits of the dead, they were still the walking invisible remnants of her friends, all she wanted was for them to gain some peace and to be able to move on.

"What can I do to help you all?"

Chumpy Tuppence moved forward, her hot pants almost glowing in the half-light of the room, her breasts pressurising the buttons on her silky blouse to almost 'popping-point' as she cleared her throat to speak.

"We need to leave limbo; we need to sort out the person who's done this to us and we need to have some form of retribution and closure. We need to have vengeance for what's been done to us and put ourselves to rest."

Melanie nodded, knowing where this was heading.

"We need to find out who this guy that had the party was and revenge ourselves."

Chapter 13: 'If You Leave Me Now'

When Grease was actually THE word

It took the world by storm, both in the cinema's and on the music charts – not to mention the posters adorning kids' walls all over the globe.

In 1978 'Grease' was truly the word and it introduced a new form of entertainment to children, the musical. The concept was already loved and adored by their parents and grandparents having been brought up on the likes of 'The Sound of Music', 'South Pacific' and 'West Side Story' amongst many, but this was on a different level.

The film featured cool kids, cool gangs, and even cooler songs, which filled the charts and the TV shows of the time.

Every boy wanted to be a 'T-Bird' and every girl wanted to be in the 'Pink Ladies'.

John Travolta of TV's 'Welcome Back Kotter' headed the male cast as Danny Zuko and Olivia Newton-John chart star and Eurovision entry for the UK starred as Sandy Olsson, starring as the star-crossed lovers in a modern interpretation of 'Romeo and Juliet' or 'West Side Story' if you're comparing it in the musical context.

The film and the songs were ingrained in the minds of anyone around at the time and the film has gone on to regularly be praised as the greatest and most loved musical of all time, rightly so...

******

Kang was sat in his lounge at the hall. He was reading through the Financial Times, checking his stocks and shares, carefully monitoring how much more he had increased his wealth in the last few days.

'*All is good in the world of 'MY' finance,*' he thought to himself as he worked out the tens of thousands that his company's profits had increased in the last few days.

He had also started to show some interest in a new record shop, which had originally opened in a tiny outlet in Notting Hill Gate, which had been a little too 'hippy' for Kang in the layout of the store, plus they had mostly specialized in 'Krautrock' bands such as Holger Czukay's Can, Faust, Popol Vuh and Amon Düül II, which wasn't his favourite style of music. They had recently moved their base to upstairs from a shoe shop on Tottenham Court Road, which seemed much more upmarket and important; but was he really interested in investing in a company that had decided to call themselves '*Virgin*'?

He had spoken to the joint owners and found that Richard appeared to be the most approachable, but was he really interested in it or not? For Kang, investments were all about making money and he felt that they would need to improve their work ethic a great deal if they were to take off.

"Mr. Kang, I have news for you," announced #1 as she entered the room, a very pleased look on her face as she crossed the parquet flooring, her leather boots tapping on the wooden surface, echoing around the room, and reverberating off the walls, as she walked with meaning, to tell Kang what she had learned.

"Tell me more," Kang replied, as he sat forward and placed the FT down on the table next to his leather armchair that had been relaxing in, picking up his glass of water and taking a sip before she began to speak.

"I know where we will be able to encounter the Moist woman and hopefully help her, like we did her friends, to disappear and in doing so, eradicate our problems."

Kang clapped his hands together, the final part of the jigsaw, the piece that they would need to eliminate, was hopefully almost in their grasp. The silver rings on his fingers clinked as his hands came together twice more.

"Spill the news now, I'm desperate to hear what you have learnt of the whereabouts of this woman."

#1 cleared her throat before she began, feeling that this announcement was going to be a very important one and enough to increase her wages and the reputation of her crew.

"I have found out, by searching the funeral announcements, that there will be a mass service for all the casualties of the Golden Palace blaze. The service and the burials will be at the South Essex Crematorium in Romford, next week on the 20th February. I'm sure that the Moist woman will be there as she will most definitely want to pay her respects to her fallen friends."

"Good, good, good," smiled Kang, "make sure that you remove this potential witness. I'm not sure if she knows anything or if she's trying to consider what happened to her friends or probe into the reason for the fire, but we need to remove her from the scene, then I will be more than pleased with your efforts."

#1 smiled, she felt that they were achieving something, and she was going to make the point of heading to the funeral herself with possibly #7, this kind of event would need to be covert, and a rapid knife attack would be easier than trying to muffle a gun shot, even with a silencer.

"Thank you, sir, I will arrange for a colleague to go with me, and we shall end this part of the story and allow your continued progression onwards through Soho."

With that, #1 bowed to Kang and left the room, at the same speed with which she'd came in, determined to seek out #7 and plan their way of finishing off Melanie Moist the following week.

'It might prove to be a difficult hit,' she thought to herself, due to the amount of people there, though that element could act in their

favour as people may not notice them and they could sneak in, finish her off and exit before their attack had even been detected.

But above all #1 had an air of confidence, as she headed along the corridor towards the stairs to their basement headquarters.

Back in the lounge Kang went back to his Financial Times, smiling – tomorrow was going to be a good day.

Chapter 14: 'Vincent'

The Vietnam War

The Vietnam War was one of the longest conflicts of the 20ᵗʰ Century, beginning on 1ˢᵗ November 1955 to a final ceasefire - with the fall of Saigon - on 30ᵗʰ April 1975, 19 years, 5 months, 4 weeks, and a day.

The war was the second of the Indochina wars and was fought between North and South Vietnam. The North of Vietnam gained support from China, with South Vietnam gaining the full support of the US and many anti-communist allies.

The casualties of the war were catastrophic, with 1,353,000 people dying in total, with 282,000 of them being from the US and allied troops.

The American ground war began on the 8ᵗʰ March 1965 with the arrival of 3,500 US Marines landed in South Vietnam, by the December of the same year this figured had increased to just short of 200,000 Marines, a significant figure, but one that seemed more than appropriate at the time.

As the war continued though, the morale of the US army collapsed and the desertion rates amongst soldiers on the ground increased four times from 1965 to 1966.

From 1970 the US began to withdraw troops, as did Australia and New Zealand who were nearer to the conflict that any of the American enlisters.

'The Deer Hunter' and 'Apocalypse Now' were released at cinemas in the '70s and both give extensive coverage of the barbarism and futility of the war – both went on to win many awards and are considered classics, mostly due to their casting, editing, direction and realism.

******

I t was two weeks since the explosion at the Golden Palace and the event had previously graced the newspapers for a few days but had then been forgotten by the media and press, as most less than newsworthy items do. When the explosion had first happened, the story had hit all the front pages –

Was it an IRA terrorist attack?

When would they own up to it?

Why had this place been chosen?

Were the owners of the Golden Palace anti-IRA?

But when it had come out a few days into the investigation that the explosion had been due to a gas-line explosion, the interest in the story began to wane and by the third day, the interest in the strip clubs demise had dwindled, with the hacks of Fleet Street splashing other stories - which were more exciting - across the front page of their papers – scandal and chaos sells papers and this was no longer an interesting story to keep the general public interested.

Melanie had been staying at the home of Byron and Nancy ever since and they had been the perfect hosts. She'd had a few snide comments directed at her by Miriam, when she'd left the house to head into Romford for some clothes shopping, but to Melanie it was water off a ducks back, having had to endure much worse when she was still at the club.

She had gone into Romford to buy some clothes for the funerals of her friends - which were all being held, '*en masse*', on the same day at the South Essex Crematorium and Cemetery in Romford. It was going to be a big affair, with hopefully a massive send off and a fitting tribute to her family from the club.

But the day of the funeral would be the following day, the 20th of February and it would help her to put closure on the events of the last two weeks and to hopefully help all her friends out of 'limbo' and go on to something much better, something much more relaxed than hanging out in this netherworld.

Chapter 15: 'Drift Away'

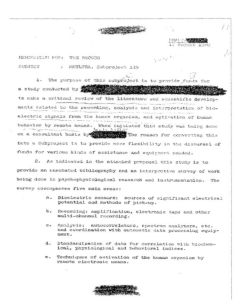

MK-Ultra – Mind Bending stuff…

Beginning in the fifties in - 1953 to be precise – MK-Ultra was an illegal experiment into mind control adopted by the CIA, which finally came to an end in 1973.

Designed to work with hallucinogenic drugs such as LSD, sleep deprivation, hypnosis, and electric shock treatment, this was the worse way of interrogating captive and had been derived from the Nazi death camps and Japanese prisoner of war camps of WWII.

Over 7,000 American war veterans took part in these experiments and took part all over the country, from military bases to college campus to prisons.

The whole purpose of MK-Ultra was looking into mind control, specifically for use against the communist bloc countries – Russia, China, North Korea etc. The CIA set up detention camps in Germany, the Philippines and Japan, where they could experiment on these mind control methods, without being prosecuted for their 'research projects'.

Frank Olson was one of the known deaths at the hand of the project, where he jumped out a window in the 1950's during a bout of psychosis, having been administered LSD without being aware of it – but his family believed that he was murdered.

Well known people who were possibly part of the MK-Ultra experiment included James 'Whitey' Bulger (mobster), Ted Kaczynski (the Unabomber) and Charles Manson.

Plus, the well-known cases who were part of Government LSD experimentation included the author Ken Kesey ('One Flew Over the Cuckoo's Nest'), Allen Ginsberg and Robert Hunter – all these experiments took place at Stanford University.

After 'Watergate' most of the files relating to MK-Ultra were destroyed, but 20,000 files were missed filed and escaped destruction causing claims and cases.

The CIA claim that the MK-Ultra programme is no more.

******

It was the morning of the funeral and it was still February so the weather was still pretty miserable as Melanie rolled over in her bed and came face to face with Nat King Cock.

"Morning there sleepy head," he crooned at her, his voice still carrying a lilting, sing-song quality to it – even though he wouldn't be performing live anymore, it didn't seem to stop him.

Looking around the room it looked like the waiting room at Gloucester Road coach station, all the spirits were sat on the floor, lying on the chest of drawers by the window, standing up asleep in a row and snoring at the bottom of the bed, resting on the covers.

"Morning Nat," she said, between yawns and eye rubbing, "it'll be a big day for all of us today and we'll have to see how many people turn up; I gotta feeling it'll be very busy."

Melanie had only attended three funerals in her life so far - her grandfather, her grandmother and one of her best friends, who had died young from cystic fibrosis when she had just finished secondary school and so it was an incredibly sad farewell.

Her grandfather had died when she was only ten years old, in the senior year of Primary School. He had been of quite elderly, just having celebrated his 80th birthday and so it had been expected - though not so soon - but it still came as a bit of a shock, as losing a close family member always does. The service had been in a small slightly overgrown cemetery and unlike most funerals that her family had attended; this one had been a burial and not a cremation.

It had been in the afternoon, just after lunchtime, though no one had taken lunch, all saving themselves for the buffet at the wake after the service. The weather had taken a turn for the worse as the heavens opened and a torrential downpour came directly down on the graveyard and from the sunnier weather in the far distance, it seemed to be just on their service, which was crueler than she could have imagined.

As the vicar gave his sermon the rain poured down and the thoughts of this day had stuck in Melanie's memory forever. The lashing storm rained down on the lid of the coffin, like a thousand tiny tapping hammers. As all the mourners stood around - their heads bowed in sadness - the vicar threw some earth onto the coffin lid, which he then passed some to her father to repeat, as part of the service.

That funeral hadn't been the best one to go to - especially for her first, but then none are ever very nice, but today was going to be the worst, today would be the funeral to end all funerals - 12 people all buried at the same time, all buried in the same cemetery and not one of them was going for cremation.

It was going to be a very long service because most of the families were choosing a song, so it was looking to be two hours or two hours plus for the whole combined services to be completed.

After the service there would of course be the '*small-talk*' session.

Speaking to all her friend's families, but not telling them that she could see them all around the open graves would be awkward, especially for the fear of her friend's families thinking that she'd gone mental and was losing the plot. Since all her friends had died and her life as she knew it had ended in the fireball that caused the destruction of the Golden Palace, the families would think that she was struggling to cope.

Looking around the room, her rag-tag group of 'friends' were now all wide-awake.

Her now, ex-work colleagues, were each beginning to contemplate the thoughts of attending their own funerals - a prospect that would be difficult to comprehend for any person. Their once jovial and pleasant faces were now gloomy, with their mouths turned down giving extra emphasis to their sadness.

"Cheer up folks, isn't it still a positive step in the right direction for you?" Melanie questioned, knowing that she would still need to do something about the criminal mastermind that had caused this?

"I don't want to see my family so upset," sobbed Ophelia, floating by the window, her feet hovering five inches above the bedroom carpet. "My children will be devastated," chipped in Curly.

"Mine too," agreed Something, wiping a solitary tear away, with a ghostly handkerchief.

Melanie looked around them all. It was difficult to see all her friends so upset, but it couldn't be helped now. She'd have to do her utmost after the funeral, to cheer them all up and keep them entertained, which would be the hardest part of the day, because although her friends had all died, they were in fact still with her, even though she was the only one able to actual see and interact with them. Though how long they would be around after the service was anybody's guess, with them all hoping to pass on completely and end this halfway-house situation between heaven and Earth.

"I'll do what I can," Melanie continued, "I've written a little speech too, so wish me luck and let's get this situation laid to rest forever."

As Melanie jostled with the spirits to get near the mirror - elbowing her way in so that she could see - she realised that she could move freely through her friends, as if their bodies were made of air.

As one arm moved through her chest, all she could feel was a slight movement and an icy shudder as they went right through her – this would take a lot of getting used to, she thought to herself as she began to brush her long dark locks and start to apply her make-up.

Sitting naked in the bedroom shouldn't really have been that much of a problem to Melanie, having been seen naked by most of her friends before, but that was from a distance. It was much different being up on stage and parading around naked or semi-naked in front of the spotlights, but being this close to people, dead or not, was slightly off putting and more than a little embarrassing.

"All turn your backs now; can't a lady get a little privacy in her boudoir?"

With that, a chill breeze blew through the room as all the ex-Golden Palace crew, turned away from Melanie, some then facing into the bedroom, others looking straight at bare walls or out of the window. Melanie brushed her hair once more as she practiced her internment speech in her head, which would hopefully fill a few minutes in the service, covering how they had all been one big happy family at the club and how they had all watched out for one another.

Brushing red nail varnish from her cuticles to her nail tips, she looked at herself in the mirror.

'Beauty is in the eye of the beholder' as they say, but Melanie couldn't see what others saw in her appearance.

She was slightly taller than average height for a woman at 5'9" tall, her facial features were soft and attractive, not carved from pure alabaster like some models appeared to be and her legs were long, but 'soft and cuddly', making men want to run their hands all over them from ankle to crotch – and a lot of men had tried over the years, some getting removed from the club, if it was during a performance.

But it was her breasts that were her main attraction and the items that gained her the most popularity plus the ability to gain more tips on the stripping circuit than anyone else in the history of the Soho sex scene.

She was a woman of larger than average size, weighing in at a much appreciated 44EE, which made her stand out from many of the other ladies on the circuit, which was why she was relied upon to bring in the punters week after week and to make sure that they turned up again and again, often checking ahead to see if she was performing or working as she liked to think of it - because it was only a job.

As she did her 'striptease in reverse' getting ready and putting on her clothes for the funeral, she thought about what was she going to do next? How was she going to cope with no job? What was going to be her next position? How was she going to make ends meet and how was she going to bring in finances to pay for a new place to live?

All these thoughts spun around in her head, as she coupled the clasps on her bra and pulled her little black dress on over her head, zipping the back up with her arms at angles behind her.

She stopped and looked at herself in the mirror. '*You look pretty good*' she thought to herself, '*not bad for someone who has just had all her friends die in a fireball of an inferno and you will be accompanying them all to their own funeral.*'

"Fuck it," she exclaimed as she caught one of her fingernails in the zip, part of it 'pinging off' across the room, flying through Nat's chest and rebounding off the wall.

"Everything ok," came a call from the hallway, as Nancy came out of her bedroom, getting ready for another shift at work - this time at the A&E department at Old Church Hospital, due to a shortage of staff because of a local strike over the usual pay and conditions.

"Everything's fine, just a cosmetic malfunction," she replied, muttering under her breath about needing to repaint her nails now, before she prepared herself to leave.

"You can all turn around now, I'm decent again, well as respectable as I can be," Melanie whispered, knowing that Nancy might be still out on the landing.

Melanie felt a slight icy breeze as all her 'spirit friends' floated around to face her once more, all smiling, with some giving her the thumbs up for her appearance, which boosted her confidence, ahead of the funeral.

"So, you think I look okay then?" she asked, giving a twirl 'a la Anthea Redfern' and fishing for compliments and getting plenty in return, as each of her friends told her how fine she looked, how smart her clothes were and that she would wow the people in attendance, especially when she made her speech, after a few of the songs and prayers had been said over the course of the service.

"You look fabulous, you're going to do us all proud," said Tuna Tunnel, her arms flailing around to emphasis her point, "it's going to be an awesome funeral, it's a shame that we aren't going to be there."

"You will be there you pillock," replied Crusty Bucket, shaking her blonde bob, "there's no way that we're going to miss our greatest performance!"

Melanie looked at the crowd; it was going to be a remarkable afternoon that was for sure, the strangest of all afternoons, for each one of them.

******

Across the other side of Essex at Whitchitley Hall, #1 and #7 were squeezing themselves into their leather trousers and jackets and then making their way up from the basement to the entrance hall, heading for the main doors. Walking across the gravel path, kicking up a dusty trail, they headed towards the area where the staff's cars were parked and headed for their black Ford Cortina Mk III.

The car was immaculate and had been polished to within an inch of its metal and enamel painted life by #4 (the karate expert), as she had brushed on and brushed off the wax, as oriental martial arts experts would.

#1 pulled the keys out of her pocket and slid them into the lock, turning them with a fluid motion, the keys becoming an extension of her hand and opening the door to get in – she'd be driving and #7 would be the passenger on their trip, riding shotgun to a funeral, which for them seemed quite appropriate.

The MDS leader had informed #7 of their strategy and how they planned to go to the send-off for the Golden Palace crew, seeking out Melanie Moist, inviting her back to their car and then taking her to a secluded place, out in the countryside and finishing her off.

Today would be the day that the MDS would prove their worth and make Kang realise that they truly were – indispensable.

Chapter 16: Big Yellow Taxi

'Putting the willies up you, with 'Rentaghost'

Released first in 1976, 'Rentaghost' was a live action children's comedy TV show in a cartoon style, based around a group of ghosts from various times in history.

The first four series featured Anthony Jackson (of 'Bless This House') as Fred Mumford, a recently deceased ghost who sets up an agency where people can rent ghosts to haunt their homes and castles, but nothing ever goes to plan.

Fred is accompanied by Hubert Davenport (a Victorian gentleman) played by Michael Darbyshire and Timothy Claypole (a court jester) played by Michael Staniforth (who wrote and sang the theme tune as well).

These were the three main characters in series one to four and from then onwards there was the introduction of Hazel the McWitch played by Scottish actress Molly Weir in series four and Nadia Popov (sneezing Dutch teleporting ghost) in series six, played by 'Coronation Street' actress Sue Nicholls (Audrey Roberts).

With the leaving of Fred and Hubert after series four, the replacements for running the business were the 'live' couple Mr. Harold and Ethel Meaker, with all the chaos that it entailed.

One of the other main characters was the pantomime horse Dobbin, which Timothy Claypole brought to life in the 1979 Christmas special and was completely unable to reverse the spell.

******

J ust a little after 2pm, the trail of hearses - all shining and black - plus funeral cars, began snaking their way through the city centre heading to Romford Cemetary in Crow

Lane. The Cemetery was opened to serve the local population in Victorian times and was quite large, covering over 25 acres.

It featured a chapel for the services and today it was going to be filled, as it only was able to house 50 mourners. With all her deceased colleague's friends and their families in attendance, it was agreed that the service would also be broadcast outside and so speakers were mounted on posts either side of the chapel entrance, so that the many people who couldn't fit inside, could listen to the proceedings, and still feel part of the congregation from the outside, and luckily for them it wasn't raining.

The weather had cheered up a little in the last few weeks and so although it was still what you'd call fresh, there was no rain, but blue skies and a small blustery breeze. The ice from the previous few weeks, where the pavements and roads had turned to slippery glass was no more, but the weather had been quite bitter, though today was a vast improvement on what had already passed.

At the head of the funeral procession was a grand horse drawn hearse, with the coffin and flowers for Biffo McGuire in the back, all viewable through the glass panels, which were clean and shined to an immaculate level.

The other hearses which followed were a much less lavish affair. The families of the strippers, the doormen and the performers, had less money to squander on what would be the final journey of their relatives and partners – times were extremely hard for some families around the London area, and the financial struggle was more than evident at this, the saddest of times.

As the parade slowly passed through the Essex streets, the crowds of onlookers stood in silence. The older men doffed their caps as the black tsunami of mourning passed through their hometown, heading towards the cemetery, their final destination.

Following the hearses was a never-ending procession of funeral cars and black cabs, carrying all the family and friends in a row to the cemetery.

Melanie was in a black cab - not exclusive enough to be in one of the Daimlers that led the procession with family members. Looking into the cab from streetside, it appeared to anyone of the hundreds of 'rubberneckers' that she was on her own in her sadness, but for Melanie it was a totally different experience.

Melanie was sat in the back of the black cab surrounded by her spirit friends. To her left was Minky Bob and Fishy, squeezed to her right were Everard Koch and Biffo McGuire. Sat opposite, jammed onto the two facing seats were Ophelia, Tuna, Crusty and Katerina. Squished onto the floor were a cross legged Chumpy, Curly and Something Fingers and Nat.

Being of another dimension and other worldly, they weren't so crushed as the living would have been, as their limbs passed through each other and as they sat entwined, they all sobbed and tried to hug each other, arms slipping through each other's spirit bodies, but the feeling was still there.

"How long until we arrive?" asked Chumpy, still in her hot pants as she would always be, sat on the floor.

"Ten minutes, there's not far to go," Melanie replied, brushing hair off her little black dress, and dragging her fingers through her hair, trying to make herself look as presentable as she could.

"Thank god, I just want this over."

Chumpy smiled up at Melanie. They were best friends, had been for what seemed like a lifetime, and she was feeling quite sad at the thought that they may not be together for much longer, once their deaths had been solved. If it was possible that she could end her existence in peace, it was what she wanted, but now she was just sad, that she was no longer alive, sad that she had been murdered and her life ended unnecessarily early and most of all, sad that she might not be able to see her friend Melanie for that much longer.

"Here we are," said the taxi driver, looking back over his shoulder at the lonely girl in the back of his cab, who had been talking to herself most of the way - nearly all the journey to the cemetery. He put it down to the fact that she was very upset due to heading out to a funeral; he got all sorts in the taxi, but sadness affected people in many ways, and he'd seen it all over the years of driving people around.

As the procession passed through the cemetery gates, the cars gradually slowed down even more, to a walking speed and eventually all pulled up outside the chapel of rest. People began to leave the cars and cabs and wait outside, making small talk and introducing themselves to all the people that they had never met before.

Funerals were not only a foundation for unbelievable sadness, grief and crying, but they were also a place for bringing people together, making new friends and acquaintances and sharing memories and thoughts of the happy times that everyone liked to remember. From passing the time finding out who the others in attendance were, to how they knew the deceased, a funeral was a bonding experience for the people in their anguish and it was a cleansing of the soul, a place to help people begin to move on. After a funeral, the people would go back to their usual lives and attempt to rebuild the emptiness that the missing person had evoked and then life goes on, life must go on.

Melanie exited the taxi, followed by her own procession of ghostly friends - observable to her, but of course completely invisible to anyone else.

The recently deceased of the Golden Palace looked around at all the people who had come to see them off. People spotted their families, all stricken in grief, and this brought them to the edge of an emotional breakdown as well. People always want to know what their funeral would be like and how many people would turn up on the actual day, but now that this band of friends were here at their final journey, they were having second thoughts and the grieving on display made the event gradually become more and more unbearable.

Melanie walked across the rough gravel path and made a bee line for Biffo's widow, it seemed appropriate as he had helped her at her time of need, and this was the time that Mrs. McGuire would need all the help she could garner. Standing near the entrance to the chapel, Mrs. McGuire was all dressed in black with a net veil across her face from her hat. She dabbed at face with an already soggy and stained cotton handkerchief, smearing the mascara around her eyes as she attempted to stem the flow of tears that were rapidly cascading down her cheeks in a salty flood of raw emotion.

"Hello Mrs. McGuire, I'm so, so sorry for your loss."

She looked up at Melanie, still finding it difficult that everyone was being so nice to her.

"That's OK Melanie and remember you can call me Pam," she replied, offering her outstretched shaking hand.

"OK Mrs. McGuire," was all that Melanie could reply, nerves already getting the better of her and she still had her speech to make yet, that was going to be the real test of the day.

"She just looks so sad," said Biffo standing at Melanie's left shoulder, "I shouldn't be leaving her on her own, she's got the brains of a child, how's she going to cope without me?" With those words, a ghostly tear dribbled down his face, sparkling in the daylight like glitter and then fading away and disappearing into nothing as he stood staring at his widow, his head shaking from side to side.

Melanie continued her walk around the mourners outside the

chapel and introduced herself to her friends' families - the widows, the brothers and sisters, the odd few children who had been taken out of school for the afternoon and finally ending with the vicar.

"Hello Father, my name's Melanie and I will be reading the eulogy today," she said, smiling through the tears that were welling up in eyes, it was a hard afternoon, and it was only going to get more difficult.

Father Thaddeus smiled at her, placing both his hands on hers, the heat from his fingers casting a glow across her and giving her an inner warmth that gradually made her feel a little better, building her confidence and knowing that she would do her friends proud.

"My child, it will all be fine, I have faith and God must have a plan for you, in that you were not part of this terrible, terrible tragedy and you live on to honour their memories and fight the good fight one day at a time."

Father Thaddeus was tall, slim, and heavily bearded, with large black framed glasses. He stared down at Melanie, putting her mind at rest and giving her a new feeling of self-assurance, knowing that the day would go ok and that she would be a beacon of light on a dark, dark day.

He smiled at Melanie, and she screwed her eyes up and looked back at him. She then realised where she recognised the priest from and that Father Thaddeus had been an occasional attendee at the Golden Palace, minus the cassock of course.

'It takes all sorts and I've seen most of them,' Melanie thought to herself as she winked at the priest, him going a little red as he blushed - getting a little hot under the dog collar.

Giving the priest another wink, she walked into the chapel and walked towards a seat in the second-row pew, as she would be making her speech part way through the service and needed to be close by.

There were vases of flowers displayed all around the walls, brightening the chapel and making the otherwise fusty building smell beautiful and fresh. The lilies gave the otherwise dull interior a lift and although lilies were traditionally a flower associated with the souls of the deceased returning to a place of peace and tranquility, they very much cheered the place up.

Melanie took her seat in the second row, on the end, with Biffo's widow and the parents of Fishy and Ophelia sat to her left, with her sat next to the aisle for easy access to the pulpit for her oration.

Her nerves were easing, but she knew that she would soon be crying, because it was a known fact that all women tended to cry at funerals and many men as well, though many of them tried to hide it. Within the hour her eyes would succumb to the salty onslaught of floods of tears, as the memories flowed, and the coffins were placed at the front of the chapel by the small legion of pallbearers. The local funeral service had to hire in extra staff to cover the funeral from several of their other branches across the length and breadth of Essex, as they didn't have sufficient cover in their one local branch and twelve coffins took a lot of carrying plus the ushering and greeting guests obviously was highly important at such a large service.

As the church gradually began to fill Melanie flicked through the order of service to see when she would be up to speak.

There was an opening introduction by Father Thaddeus and then the song 'All Things Bright and Beautiful', followed by a brief history of the families and some witty anecdotes that the Father had been passed by relatives and friends, next came a few prayers and a reading from the bible by one of the children from Biffo's family. She noticed that her 'piece' was straight after that and just before a selection of music was played over the speakers, including Slade,

Candi Statton, The Rubettes, Andrew Gold and many more – finishing with the song 'Make It With You', which had always been a favourite to play in the club when it was quiet, and no one was performing.

The pews gradually filled and the area at the back of the chapel appeared to be crammed with people standing. Looking around Melanie noticed several regular punters at the back, attending to give their final farewells to not only the performers and staff who had passed away, but also the club which had become a major part of their lives.

As Melanie continued to look around the inside of the building, she noticed the spirits of her friends all hovering at the front, around the coffins. A few of them were wailing and sobbing their hearts out, unable to control their emotions when watching their partners and family members at this, the saddest of times. Luckily the only person able to hear the groans from the beyond was Melanie, which made it equally hard for her, as she was getting the whole experience two-fold and had to endure the sobs and tears of both the living and the recently deceased.

It was now fifteen minutes before the service and the emotions were running high amongst all in attendance and Melanie thought back to her grandfather's funeral, which she had attended when she was only fifteen.

He had been the world to her.

He would give her lifts to school when she was late, lend her pocket money when she was short, and she would go to his flat and spend the evening in front of the TV with him and her Nana every Saturday evening – watching 'Doctor Who' with Patrick Troughton and 'Dixon of Dock Green' being TV favourites. They would have sardines on toast for supper and 'Lemon Turd' on toast as well – which was what her Nana always called it, which always made everyone laugh. Her Mum and Dad would be their too and her two sisters – Marcia and Mildred – plus her brother Marvin.

Thinking back to these times made her very sad. Her heart was broken when her parents had been killed in a hot tub accident, both electrocuted in their back garden when the pump short circuited. They had been virtually fried, ending up looking like the sardines that Nana served as the Doctor played his recorder, to help him think. It was after this incident and the funeral that her sisters and brother left the area and moved abroad – she hadn't heard from them for years and it was at gatherings like this that the memories all came flooding back, like a tsunami of grief.

She missed her siblings more than she could express in words and hoped that she would be able to see them again in the future; but the girls were together somewhere in Greece and Marvin had moved to America and was in a band somewhere in California, so without an income, it would be difficult to travel to the distances to see them.

With less than ten minutes to go to the start of the service, Melanie got her speech out of her pocket and checked it through once more. She had a full large sheet of notepaper and she had covered both sides, in large enough print so that she would be able to read it easily in front of all the friends and families. It still felt a little daunting having to stand up in front of so many people, but it was what they all deserved, and she was going to give it to them, both barrel loads.

Looking to the back of the chapel, Melanie cast her eye across the people who were unable to get seats. The throng at the back was three people deep and that didn't include the crowds outside who couldn't even squeeze into the service and would have to make do with listening on the speakers surrounding the entrance.

Melanie spotted a few people that she recognised.

There were a couple of people from the Ship and three or four bar staff from the Intrepid Fox, all dressed in their most sombre attire – black suits, white shirts, and black slick ties, they all looked suitably dressed for the day. There were also several people from the Marquee club – the DJ and the guy who ran the mixing desk and the lights for the stage. There were even several staff that she only recognised - but couldn't name - from the Hammer film studios offices on Wardour Street. There were also several people from the local shops to the Golden Palace and offices that were very nearby; it was almost like the 'Who's Who' of Soho.

But there were lots of people that she didn't recognise as well, from the several elderly pensioners sat in the final rows, before the people standing for the service, to the two Eastern European looking women clad all in leather just staring at her and further staring, which began to creep her out a little.

But not to worry, people showed their grief in different ways, and she was sure that there were people there who begrudged the fact that she was still alive and that their son, daughter, husband, sister were now no longer with them.

Five minutes to the beginning of the service and Father Thaddeus made his way down the aisle, passing all the mourners, his cassock flowing like Batman's cape, heading up the steps to his pulpit to begin the service very shortly.

Music played across the speakers, and everyone was treated to 'Vincent' by Don McLean, with the heartfelt lyrics putting most people at ease, but for many adding to the tears in abundance as well. Then as the final acoustic plucks of the guitar echoed around the chapel, Father Thaddeus cleared his throat and prepared to speak the opening words of the service.

"Good afternoon, everyone and I'd like to welcome you all to Romford Cemetery and the South Essex Crematorium. I hope that you can all hear me clearly and that the speakers are working well enough outside as we have had some problems before with the wind and mice nibbling at the cables," he began, with everyone nodding to inform him that they could all hear him loud and clear.

"This is a bit of an unusual service for me, as we don't normally have twelve people who have all passed at the same time and a mass ceremony taking place for them all at once. I can fully understand the need for this to take place for everyone on the same afternoon, as it has brought everyone together to give a remembrance service that people will talk about for years to come and the chance for us all to celebrate their lives and what they all brought to the community of Soho." Father Thaddeus smiled at the mourners and carried on with his sermon.

"For all these lives to have been destroyed in such an awful way and to leave their loved ones in such a dramatic manner is far beyond the usual grief that I witness on a day-to-day basis. But we are here today to help these brothers and sisters of the '*sex industry*' to pass on with the love of God and make their way to a better place, where they will live on forever at peace and here on earth they will live on in our thoughts and memories for evermore."

The rows of mourners dabbed at their eyes, as the thoughts that they would never see their friends or relatives again struck home and made for the start of a very sombre afternoon.

"I now would like us to turn to the first song chosen for today - which is a very uplifting one – "All Things Bright and Beautiful", if you could all stand."

With that the organ started up and the small choir – three elderly pensioners from the local congregation and two teenage boys from the local Warren Comprehensive School – stood up and began singing like their own lives depended on it. All the people in attendance sang or hummed along, some fully interested in taking part in the service and others there just to pay respect to the recently deceased.

Melanie looked around the chapel.

It was an uplifting song. It lifted everyone's spirits up and pushed them to the forefront of the chapel, pretty much like Melanie's bra, which was lifting her up and pointing her in the right direction as well. As the song came to an end, Father Thaddeus stood up at the pulpit and addressed the families and friends once more.

"Now as we know, all our recently passed friends and relatives worked together at the Golden Palace adult entertainment venue in Soho. Having never been to anywhere like that in my life, I can't draw comparisons and memories from my own experiences, but I'm sure some of the stories that I will be reading from people who had experienced this form of showbiz will give you an idea of the camaraderie and friendship that was experienced within the walls of the said venue daily."

Catching the Father's eye, Melanie winked at him, knowing different – *"the lying bugger"* she thought to herself, trying to remember exactly how many times she had seen him at their complex. As he saw Melanie staring at him, he began to blush, but it wasn't noticed by anyone else, most of them too stricken by grief to pay attention to the flushing of the priest's cheeks.

"Working in this industry one would always encounter problems," he began looking around to make sure that everyone was paying attention and hanging on his every word. "No more problems than the ones that were encountered by Minky Bob, Curly Hamilton and Something Fingers – colourful names, for colourful door staff."

Everyone sat nodding and rubbing their eyes and blowing their noses, waiting for the amusing anecdotes that would cheer them up, lightening the mood in the chapel.

"From beating up people who refused to pay for the lap dances to the punters who tried to touch the naked bodies of the exotic dancers, Minky, Curly and Something had seen and sorted it all."

Some of the more elderly people tutted at the priest's opening narrative, it being a little too violent and close to the knuckle for them to expect to hear in a church service, but Father Thaddeus was a modern priest and he felt that he needed to the roll with the punches, just like the bouncers did.

With that opening, Father Thaddeus continued with several more inappropriate and equally unlistenable stories, which had been fed to him by the congregation. After telling several more tales about the girls and their trouble getting changed in such small dressing rooms to how the club made so much money that Mr. and Mrs. McGuire would go to Acapulco each year on holiday with the profits. After fifteen minutes more of colourful and explicit stories, the congregation began to appreciate the tales and the tears turned to laughter, as the time approached for Melanie to do her speech.

Father Thaddeus smiled as he told the final tale about a missing G-String and a tube of lube and then went straight into a few prayers where everyone bowed their heads, mumbled along and then joined in with a rousing 'AMEN' at the end. Biffo's nephew Karl then came up to do a reading from the bible, trying to be uplifting, though he could barely read - despite being fifteen years old - but everyone put it down to nerves, but the truth was that he was just poorly educated and a little slow. After this Father Thaddeus stood back from the pulpit and took a seat near the choir, making space for Melanie and her memories of the Golden Palace.

Standing up and smoothing down her dress, all eyes were on Melanie as she walked down the aisle and climbed the steps up into the pulpit. As she stood behind the stone façade, all eyes were on her voluptuous chest, as several of her buttons had popped and she was revealing a little more than she should have been, especially in a house of God. Not noticing her blouse faux pas, she cleared her throat and began.

"Hello everyone, it is so nice to see you all here today, though the situation is not what we'd ever want to see, the turn out and the love in the room for all our friends and family is astounding. I have known all the people who we are here today to pay our respects to for quite a few years and it's nice to meet all their families and friends and to speak to you as well – there is a lot of love in this room, and I always thought that there would be.

I was lucky to not be working on a shift on the night of the accident and although I thank my lucky stars that I was not there, I also look to the skies and ask, '*why me?*' Why was I spared? I should have been here having respects paid to me, as well as all my friends. But perhaps I am here still for another purpose and that one today is to pay respect to the fallen heroes – and that's what they were to me – who gave their all in the name of entertainment and died doing what they loved.

We lived like a family. We all respected each other, helped each other, and looked out for each other all the time. If I was feeling down, Nat would sing me a song. If I was feeling angry Everard, would tell me a few jokes and calm me down. If I was feeling lonely, all the girls would hang around and speak to me, cheering me up with their crazy little ways."

Looking around the room, everyone was smiling and hanging on every word of Melanie's address, apart from the two women in black leather at the back, who were looking at their watches and tapping their nails on the back of the final pew. An elderly woman looked around and tutted at #1 and #7 of the Murmansk Death Squad, who were just biding their time and waiting for an opportunity to finish off the Moist woman. They both looked back at her and #7 drew a line with her nails across her throat, which terrified the woman so much, that she turned back to the front allowing the tapping to continue, trying to ignore the rude women and concentrate once more on the lady in the pulpit's speech.

"It felt like all the people I worked with were my brothers and sisters," continued Melanie, looking around and smiling at the people. "We were so '*close knit*', that we would do anything for each other, and we never fell out at all.

Work wasn't like work; it was an absolute pleasure.

We got to hang out with our '*family*', listen to great music, dance to great music, and lose our inhibitions and in doing so, we all gained in confidence and respect for each other. There were times when we would encounter awkward punters, but we always had Minky, Curly and Something at hand to help and show them the door, usually with a boot up the backside." – This line gained a lot of laughs and more tears as Curly and Something's widows hugged each other remembering their husbands and thinking about how they were going to cope now that they were gone and Minky's brother Munky, just smiled in the way that he always did.

"We stayed in the venue sometimes twenty-four hours a day, but we never tired of each other's company. We gelled together as a team and that was why no one ever left, no one ever went to work somewhere else or complained about the working conditions; it wasn't a job, it was a life choice, and we were all living the best life possible and making good money in the process.

All the girls were sensible with their money. Tuna was saving to buy a flat in Camden, Katerina was funding her college course, hoping to become a teacher eventually and Chumpy was just living a life with no worries and putting money away for that inevitable rainy day. Crusty and Fishy were talking about opening their own clothes boutique on the Kings Road in the long run and Ophelia was saving up to buy a horse for racing and they cost a lot of money. So, we all had our little plans and mine was to buy my own place eventually and the Golden Palace helped with this, it wasn't a means to an end or stop gap – it was a long-term commitment, until we reached and exceeded our life goals.

I'd also like to say a big thank you to Tommy, Bungalow and Bognor who kept the building going and are lucky, like me, to still be here today; we are very fortunate people and just so sad at the events of that evening and losing all our friends in this terrible tragedy." Tommy, Bungalow and Bognor just nodded their heads in unison at the such true words that Melanie was saying.

Melanie looked over towards the coffins at her spectral friends, who were listening intently as she spoke about them and all the love that was flowing out for them in the room. A few were standing – next to their own coffins – some were sitting on the steps in front of the curtains, which would eventually close around the coffins as they went off for cremation and Chumpy was sat in her hot pants on top of her coffin looking lost and sad. To think that they were all going to be cremated was a bit bizarre and almost an afterthought, given the fact that they had all been cremated in the fireball that had destroyed the Golden Palace in the first place.

"So, as we sit and stand here, paying our final respects, I would like to suggest instead of a prayer that we have a minute's applause to show our lost brothers and sisters what they truly meant to us and to give them the final send-off that they all deserve.

Ladies and Gentlemen, I'd like you all to stand and show your appreciation - I give you – *'The Family of the Golden Palace'*."

With that, all the mourners stood and clapped wholeheartedly and solidly for a full minute. Tears of joy and laughter reverberated around the walls of the chapel and even #1 and #7 clapped, so as not to draw attention to themselves again, as this would soon be over, they were sure.

With the clapping coming to an end, the speakers kicked back in, and Joni Mitchell's 'Big Yellow Taxi' began to play, another favourite in the rest room at the club. As Joni did her bit for conservation, Melanie went back to her seat, everyone smiling and congratulating her as she walked back to the pew where she had come from, and Father Thaddeus went back to the pulpit to give his final prayers and thoughts. Fifteen minutes later, after another hymn and the Lord's Prayer, Father Thaddeus brought the proceeding to an end and the curtains slowly began to draw around the coffins. The red velvet drapes – which nearly matched Chumpy's hotpants – snagged on the farthest of the coffins and the ushers came forward and moved the coffin slightly back enabling the curtains to completely close.

The coffins were now out of sight and so were the ghosts, to anyone but Melanie, who watched as they all stood there in shock; this had been their big send off and now it was over. People would now get on with their lives, go back to their mundane little jobs and all that was left of them were the memories and the photographs of the good times. Gradually everyone began to file out of the chapel, from the front pews to eventually the rear ones and then the people who were standing.

Melanie stood outside surrounded by the twelve spirits, them all congregating around her like she was their ringleader, which in a way she was. The wind was blowing now, and the weather had taken a turn for the worse. Melanie's long dark hair was blowing around in the breeze, making her look like a screaming banshee. As she gradually got control of her hair, she pulled it back into a ponytail and stood looking around as all the friends and family filed past, some congratulating her on her speech as they passed by her, on the way to their cars and then on to the wake.

As she looked around, she then spotted someone in the distance, by the older graves in the cemetery, she looked familiar and then she realised who she was as she walked towards her, leaving her friends hovering around the door – and some of them were doing just that, floating a few inches about the rough gravel path, because they could and that was what ghosts did.

As Melanie got near to the ancient part of the cemetery she stopped.

Then Memory Lane moved forward.

Still dressed in the clothes that she was wearing when her life was cut dramatically short at Kang's party - a short black skirt and thigh high leather boots. Her dark curly hair, framing her face and giving her a spectral appearance that was so fitting for the fact that she was now a spectre, after all.

"Hello Memory, what happened to you? Where have you been?" With that, Memory moved forward, brushed the curly hair away from her eyes and said,

"Melanie, we need to talk…"

Chapter 17: 'Babe'

'No Ring Goes, Like a Ringos Goes...'

Made originally in 1973, Ringos were a very popular brand of wheat-based snacks in Cheese & Onion and Salt & Vinegar flavour. Extremely flavoursome and very 'moreish' – they were like the crack of crisps, once you started just had to have more and more.

Still available now in some shops, but much less easily found, but as they said on the adverts – 'No Ring Goes, Like a Ringos Goes...'

******

It was a wonderful to see Memory once more, but not so good that she had passed on as well and that she looked like there was something playing on her mind in a big way, from the distraught and concerned look on her face.

"I have something awful to tell you," began Memory as she glittered and shone in the daylight, "I was killed at a party, two days before the complete destruction of the Golden Palace, all because I overheard what was really happening," she continued, the tears welling up in her eyes. She was wishing she had survived, but also feeling guilty that she hadn't stopped the sad demise of all her friends and colleagues, two days after the party where she was 'terminated'. "It's a bigger problem than the Met police and the London Fire Service think it is and it wasn't just an unfortunate accident."

Melanie looked at Memory, her stomach beginning to churn once more, having just got over the nerves of having to speak at the service   "What are you suggesting happened?" asked Melanie looking at Memory and knowing how much she missed her already, as she did all her other friends.

Memory rubbed her chin; she always did that when she was thinking, and it was one of the things that made her so attractive to the opposite sex and occasionally the same sex – that and her aura of innocence and vulnerability.

"On some of the days that you hadn't been working, I was getting chosen to perform private dances in one of the booths by a group of Chinese men from the restaurants across the way in Chinatown. They were mostly waiters and bar staff, but one evening they came with some of their 'bosses' – I'm guessing that they were the restaurant owners and managers, as they paid for the younger men's drinks and tips all night.

They talked amongst themselves as I performed - some of my more erotic moves and performances, which always gained me big tips and plenty of gratitude. Little did they know, that as they spoke, I listened, as you probably remember my stepfather was Chinese and my mother encouraged me to learn and speak Mandarin from a very early age; the younger you are the easier it is to pick up a foreign language and so from the age of six I gradually became fluent in Mandarin and a little Cantonese as well.

I listened intently to their business conversations, as I ground my bottom and gyrated my hips in their direction and occasionally in their faces. I heard their plans for expanding their business empires and how they were always looking for available properties in the Soho area," Memory continued, fading in and out, as she blended in with the gravestones.

"They mentioned the Golden Palace and that they would love to have a piece of real estate in the exact area, either the building or even better just a vacant plot of land on the same spot. And one name kept coming up all the time '*Sébastien Kang*'. It was all –

'Kang could do this so easily.'
'Kang would be the ideal man for this job.'

'Kang could sort any or all of our problems out.'

'Kang could remove the current owners and solve everything.'

The conversations went on like this all night, into the early hours of the morning and I was paid well to keep dancing and grinding away as they talked *'business'* not having a clue about my good grasp of the Chinese language. I just looked dumb all the time and smiled as they planned what to do to expand across the road further into Soho, with me taking mental notes all the time and paying close attention to what they were scheming amongst themselves.

Then a week later Kang arrived at the Golden Palace.

Again, it was another night that you weren't in, and I was called again for a long private dancing session with the oriental gentlemen. This evening there were none of the younger staff, but just the businessmen and until then, the elusive Sébastien Kang.

Kang was smart, Kang was elegant, and he paid for the other individuals drinks all night. He paid little to no attention to my dancing and from what I could understand he was there just to talk about future *'empire plans'* and how he would let nothing get in their way or stop their business expansion programme.

Our eyes never connected and I'm sure he wouldn't have been able to pick me out in an identity parade, just a young white stripper, like any of the others in the club – which I was very happy with, because I had the beginnings of a plan forming in my mind as I go-go danced my way through another tune."

Melanie was intrigued with the way the story was being told. She trusted Memory implicitly and had total faith in all that she was relaying to her, and it felt like the direction the information was heading, was that the 'fatal accident' at the Golden Palace, might not have been one after all.

"So, I listened attentively, taking in all the information that they were spilling, and I was beginning to form a plan. I was going to speak to you about it in more detail, but we seemed to be working opposite shifts to each other all the time and so I never got the chance," she said, as Melanie nodded – they hadn't seen that much of each other recently and now she'd be seeing a lot less of her, especially as the club was no more.

Memory wiped a tear from her eye, as she carried on with her story, getting to the crux of the matter, her confrontation with Kang.

"I was then invited to an extremely high-class party at Whitchitley Hall in Sussex. The Hall is the home of Kang, and this was where I was going to confront him about his plans for the Golden Palace. I had planned on speaking to him alone, but he was never alone there - he was the centre of attention, and everyone wanted to speak to him and be his friend, his wealth appeared to do that to people, especially the young girls at his shindig.

But what I forgot to mention was that I had a gun, an MP5, which I had taken from my stepfather's house. God knows what he was doing with such a high calibre weapon, but I guess it was just for protection and to ward off any would-be burglars. Mother was always paranoid about things like that, but she wouldn't have queried how he had acquired the weapon and if he would ever use it, things like that terrified her. He had lived in some very dangerous and dodgy suburbs and ghettos around the world and so I didn't really query where he had obtained it from. I was sure that he knew a lot of unsafe and untrustworthy individuals, so getting a weapon like that or any firearm probably wasn't a problem for him at all; if you knew the right unprincipled people in the underground network of a city, then anything was possible."

Staring at her, nodding, and trying not to look too shocked, Melanie struggled to take in all the info that she was being fed.

Growing up in a nice locality, with nice neighbours and the most loving and doting parents, she obviously never had a life like Memory, which sounded more like a plot of a movie than a friend's childhood.

"So, knowing what he was up to I attended the party, with my plan to stop it."

"What was his idea?" asked Melanie, fearing the answering that was coming.

"He planned to blow up the Golden Palace."

Chapter 18: 'Barracuda'

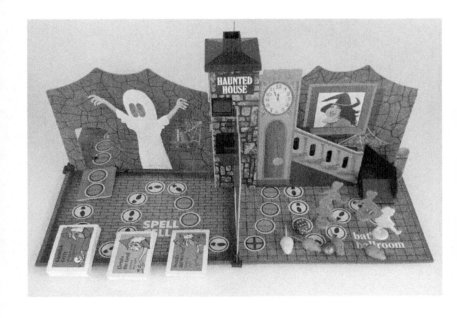

'Ghoulish Gerty Drops It Down the Chimney'

'Haunted House' was released for the first time in 1971 by the Denys Fisher company, this was a children's board game based around making your way around a haunted house and avoiding getting struck by a 'Whammy Ball' – essentially a ball bearing – which Ghoulish Gerty would drop down the chimney if you ended up picking up that card. Basing itself around the popularity in ghosts, witches and general spookiness that had been brought into the mainstream by "Scooby Doo', this game was always going to be a hit and that was exactly what it proved itself to be. Unlike other board games, such as 'Monopoly' or 'Cluedo', this game had a 3D board and needed to be slotted together before play could commence. The playing surface was divided up into four rooms (Broom Room, Spell Cell, Witchin Kitchen, Bats Ballroom) and you went around the board, with the goal being to climb up the staircase and end the game, if you hadn't already been turned into a plastic mouse or hit by the ball.

******

Standing just outside the chapel, #1 and #7 watched intently as Melanie Moist – the women that they were about to take on a little trip – appeared to be standing in amongst the graves talking to herself. They put it down to the stress of the day and waited patiently for more of the guests to leave, the quieter the better.

As the guests all filed out of the chapel, they headed to their cars and gradually, minute by minute, the cemetery emptied and got much quieter.

The final person to leave the chapel was the Priest, Father Thaddeus, who popped on his trilby hat, slid his Meerschaum pipe between his already pursed lips and walked off in a jaunty fashion towards his Morris Minor, which was parked 30 yards from the entrance. As he got to his car, he turned around and looked across the crumbling older gravestones, noticing the Moist woman seemingly in deep conversation with herself?

"Is everything OK?" he called over to her, as she gave him a thumbs up and shouted, "ALL GOOD, THANKS FOR YOUR HELP TODAY."

Father Thaddeus nodded a quick thank you, hopped into his vehicle and within seconds started up and sped out the cemetery gates, heading home for a rest or perhaps to another strip club, in disguise...

Melanie turned back to Memory and said,

"So, you know 100% that it was this Kang that planned to blow up the Golden Palace? It seems like quite a drastic course of action. If he had that much money, surely, he could have spoken to Biffo and made him an offer that he couldn't refuse or otherwise ignore?"

Memory shook her head, her dark curls fluttering and flickering as they went in and out of focus, as the fading light of the afternoon shone through her.

"He would never make an offer. From what I've seen of his business acumen, it's all TAKE. TAKE.. TAKE... He's not the kind of man who would take no for an answer either and if you ever met him, you'd understand what I mean. He's ruthless and not up for any form of negotiating and I'm sure from what I've heard, he's dealing in many dodgy business plans all over the capital and the surrounding areas. He has his sticky little finger in many grubby little pies and before long he will be caught out, because I've heard that the Met are looking into some of his exploits already – his colleagues spoke about this in the club, whilst I was performing for them. It's amazing what you can eavesdrop on, when they don't think that you can understand their language."

Taking a deep breath Memory carried on, "One of the worst things I also heard, was that they were planning on grabbing some of the girls via '*human trafficking*' and shipping them on cargo planes to Hong Kong to work in clubs there, whether they had the inclination to or not. They had already planned to drug and kidnap Katerina, Crusty and Tuna and if it hadn't been for the destruction of the Golden Palace and their untimely end, they would have been dancing now in an opium induced nightmare in a club in Hong Kong owned by Kang Sr. with no way of getting home or knowing where they were or what they were doing due to the constant topping up of their drug levels."

Melanie's jaw dropped, the situation was bad, but it seemed even worse than she had initially expected it to be – it was so much easier when they all thought that it was a gas leak.

Byron and Nancy had been so helpful putting her up at their place, and he had been investigating the explosion with the local police and they all thought that the leak was the most likely of conclusions.

"So, this is a worldwide operation then?" continued Melanie, "it's not just a little club in Soho having an accident? It's a planned bombing, kidnapping and if it went to court would it be involuntary manslaughter or not? This is a more complicated case than I was expecting, and all the guys and girls are depending on me to sort this out."

"It's a nightmare" Memory agreed.

Melanie nodded, it was a nightmare, and she was the one, with the aid of her ghostly chums left to sort it out. It was like an episode of '*Scooby Doo*' made real, with the ghosts on the side of the good guys for once and everyone would have gotten away with their lives intact, if it wasn't for those meddling Chinese gangsters!!!

"Ok then Memory, what do you suggest that we do? It's late here now and the funeral crowd has left, there's only us and those lot over there," she motioned towards the group of twelve ghosts still standing outside the entrance to the chapel, still in limbo and not knowing where they were going or what they should be doing. All the spectres waved back at them, none of them having seen Memory for a while since she disappeared.

Then Melanie noticed that her ghostly friends weren't alone. In amongst them were two women, dressed all in black and looking more than a little noticeable as they weren't see-through, they were living breathing people and they were heading their way, walking slowly across the rough gravel path, and heading directly towards the older part of the cemetery, exactly where they were chatting.

"I know exactly who these two are," said Memory worriedly, "these are two of the people who killed me at the party and I'm guessing that they are coming for you, loose ends and all that."

Melanie nodded as the two women continued their approach, getting closer with each stride of their shiny leather legs and boots.

"We know you are Melanie Moist?" The taller of the two asked, "you need to come with us, we have someone who wants to have a word with you, about your future or possibly the lack of it."

Chapter 19: 'Refugee'

"My God, you're German…"

A rollicking war adventure, concerning the plot by a crack troupe of sixteen Nazi paratroopers who fly into England and kidnap Churchill, when he is at a weekend conference in peaceful Berkshire. With a story that begins in Germany and goes via Jersey to a sleepy hamlet in England, the German soldiers disguise themselves as Polish paratroopers on manoeuvres in the English countryside, which happens to be the village next to the country house where Winston Churchill is spending the weekend. Lasting an action packed 2hrs and 15 mins, it's one of the best war films released in the 1970's with believable plot and a more than adequate group of actors. The cast list is huge including Michael Caine (Col. Kurt Steiner), Donald Sutherland (Liam Devlin), Robert Duvall (Colonel Radl), Jenny Agutter (Molly Prior), Donald Pleasance (Heinrich Himmler), Anthony Quayle (Adm. Wilhelm Canaris), Larry Hagman (Col. Clarence E. Pitts), Treat Williams (Capt. Harry Clark) and Judy Geeson (Pamela Verecker).

******

Rabbing hold of Melanie by the collar of her jacket, #1 roughly manhandled her in the direction of their black Cortina, giving her no chance to argue or kick up a fuss. The only thing that they couldn't see was the trail of thirteen spirits following her. It was like she was the Pied Piper of Soho, and all her spiritual friends would follow her wherever she went. Melanie was their natural born leader, and she was also their only chance at getting some peace and escaping this world forever.

As they walked along, they were all asking questions and querying what was happening with the two strangers in black.

"Where are we going now?" asked Biffo.

"Who are these two bitches?" queried Tuna.

"Why are they dragging you away?" inquired Katerina.

"Are they taking us in their car?" probed Fishy.

They were certainly a quizzical bunch of friends, you could give them that, but they had every right to know and so did she, Melanie thought to herself, as they dragged her along the gravel path towards their transport for the day.

The garage at Whitchitley was filled with cars, mostly black, but this car was #1's favourite and so she always chose it – if it was available - when she went out on trips and errands and business meetings for Kang.

"Hi, I'm Melanie, but you've already told me that," she smiled, neither of her captors even cracking a grin. "Where are we going? I was planning on going to see my Nana in an hour or so, you'll probably guess that I haven't got that much time to spare, and she will be needing her supper."

Her kidnappers looked at her and the shorter of the two just said in an accented voice "more walking, less talking," as she was forcibly dragged towards the car.

Arriving at the car, Melanie was pushed into the back and #1 hopped in the front, with #7 sitting in the rear with Melanie, keeping a close eye on her – if she escaped there would be hell to pay with Kang, knowing what his temper could be like at times.

The engine kicked in as #1 fired it up and they slowly began to drive out of the cemetery. The car – again to onlookers – would have looked empty, one in the front and two in the back, with not much going on, but in Melanie's vision it was totally different again.

Squeezed in the front next to the leather clad driver were Memory and Katerina, on the back sat were Chumpy, Tuna, Crusty, Fishy and Ophelia and squeezed unceremoniously in the boot were Minky, Curly, Something, Biffy and Everard. Riding on the roof and singing all the way was Nat King Cock, still the king of the crooners and as always, having a fantastic time and not giving a damn about where they were going.

The Thirteen Ghost Express was heading along at just over seventy miles an hour with a direct route to Whitchitley Hall in mind, no stops on the way, no toilet breaks unless necessary and time was of the essence, they certainly didn't want to keep Kang Jr. waiting for them to eventually arrive or they would have to suffer the consequences of his violent and angry tantrums.

"I'm all squeezed up here," moaned Katerina.

"You're squeezed up, you should try being in the boot," called Biffo from the back of the car, as they raced along the roads out of Essex, and slowly passing south of London, as they headed onwards towards Sussex.

"Quit moaning, it won't be that long I'm sure," said Melanie to her friends whose limbs were all intertwined, in and out of each other's bodies.

"What did you say?" asked #7, dragging one of her knives out of her pockets and waving it in her direction.

"Nothing just talking to myself," she replied looking at all her ghostly friends around her and shrugging.

"I can't be bothered with this nonsense," said Memory as she grabbed hold of the knife and began to move it towards #7, by way of her own hand, like a stripper poltergeist taking control of the situation. "What the fuck???" screamed #7 as she looked at the large knife coming towards her face.

#1 looked in the rear-view mirror and could just see her colleague looking like she was going to stab herself, unlike Melanie who was witnessing an even more terrifying sight, her friend controlling the woman in blacks' hand, from beyond the grave!

With that Memory forced the blade of the six-inch knife straight into #7's eye socket and the arterial spray coated the inside of the Cortina in a blood red glaze, as the knife sliced and diced through her ophthalmic artery in her right eye. With a crunching and grinding sound as the blade scraped around, #7 screamed bloody hell as she bled out all over the car.

As #1 tried to find a place to pull in and stop the car, in the back #7 continued to repeatedly stab herself in the eyes - both eyes now - having made a sliced mash up of the right eye and now she'd moved onto the left.

Memory was in full swing, and no one would be able to stop her, because no one could see her, apart from Melanie and the other twelve friends, but it was Melanie that was now coated from head to toe in a deep red coating, with the blood still spraying from the woman in black's eye sockets, as Memory went onto slicing her face to ribbons.

"Take that you bitch," screamed Memory as she continued to slash at the woman's face, controlling her own hand to do the damage. "You thought you could get rid of me," she screeched, "now I'm getting rid of you!!! Permanently!!!"

By now the inside of the car was plastered from ceiling to floor in the woman in black's blood and she was slumped back against the seat, passed out and rapidly on the way to bleeding to death. As Melanie tried to move, she slid around on the seat, the bloody coating making the leather seats incredibly slippery.

By now #7's face resembled a crisscross pattern of slices and hacks, and blood was everywhere as she raised her hand for one final time – via the aid of Memory – and sliced straight across her throat. Her jugular tore and the flesh of her neck split, becoming a gaping opening in a bloody ragged tear, with a new fountain of thick gushing, frothing blood spraying from the back of the car, into the front, all over #1 and completely coating the windscreen in plasma.

Covered in blood and unable to see, #1 lost control of the car and crashed into a sycamore tree at the side of the road in Barnes on Queen's Ride, which was part of the B306 close to Gipsy Lane.

As the woman in black and red staggered out of the car, all the spirits followed her and watched as she wobbled at the side of the road from the crash. Melanie, who had luckily been wearing her seat belt attempted to leave the car unaided. '*Clunk-click*' she thought to herself once more, as she unbuckled herself and climbed out of the back of the car and walked towards the dazed and confused woman, arm against the tree, wiping blood from her eyes and hair, by the side of the road.

"What happened back there?" the woman asked Melanie in a heavy Eastern European accent, "what happened to my friend?"

"I think she got her comeuppance and I'm sorry to tell you, but I think that you might be next."

As Melanie finished speaking, she watched as Memory – still on a bloody rampage – lifted a very hefty and thick tree branch and ran at #1 with it.

#1 screamed as she watched a large piece of tree levitate itself slowly up off the ground and then speedily come towards her, as fast as a speeding arrow.

As she skreiched loudly, Memory slammed the branch down

through her teeth, smashing all the front ones and jamming it deep into her throat. Wedging the gap in her esophagus, #1 began to suffocate, scratching at her neck as she struggled to breathe, her face gradually turning a deep shade of blue, as her airways were closed off.

As she began to die, she looked at Melanie and, in the light, she didn't seem to be alone. It looked like she was standing there with another dozen people and they were all clear and translucent, but she put it down to the lack of air and hallucinating as she began to drift out of consciousness, eventually passing away at the side of the road.

"Well, that was exciting," hollered Memory, clearly pleased with herself, but all her friends appeared to be in total shock at what they'd just witnessed. "If we are going to save Melanie and sort out this Kang fella, then that's the way to do it," she chuckled to herself, clearly in a state of shock at her actions, not knowing that she even had the strength or impetus to carry out such a violent act.

"So, what do you suggest we do now then?" Melanie asked Memory and when she received no reply from her, she looked to the others, who all shrugged their shoulders and looked to Chumpy, who was always full of good ideas.

"I guess we go to the country house where we were being taken and see this Kang dude, it's the only plan we have, and we all want to get sorted and out of here, I'm sure."

Melanie looked around the semi-circle of friends and they all nodded in agreement, they all wanted to leave this 'limbo' and get their murders avenged and sorted, for once and for all and then they might get some peace.

Looking down at her clothes, Melanie looked like she'd been in an abattoir. She was soaked in blood from the dead woman in the car, from head to toe. The only place that was clean was the gap between her breasts, where they had been squeezed together in the car during the bloodbath.

"Ok then, let's move the other body out of the car and dump them both in the river, they won't turn up for weeks or if they do, they'll appear further along the Thames – just a suggestion?"

All of Melanie's friends agreed to her suggestion and acting like the poltergeists they now were, they helped move the bodies, weigh them down with pebbles, stones, and bricks and tossed them into the Thames, the bodies sinking without trace, for now; but if the bodies resurfaced in a few days or weeks, they would be long gone and the local Old Bill would have no chance in making the connection to a woman on her own, who had only recently left a funeral.

'Having friends like these can be an advantage at times," she thought to herself as she hiked back up the path to where they had left the car.

Being sensible she had filled a large lemonade bottle that she'd found at the side of the river with water and brought it back to the car and sluiced down the inside windows, until she was able to see out them. The windows of the car were slightly tinted and so any blood residue that was still anywhere on the glass couldn't be noticed from the outside – the inside was a different matter.

Blood was sticky all over the seats and had pooled up in congealed puddles in all the footwells of the car. The inner doors were painted red and the seats in the front, the headrests, the ashtray, and even the radio were all plastered in gore, sticky and tacky to the touch. Melanie then dropped the bombshell.

"I hope you all realise that I'm unable to drive, I've never learnt." With that, Something Fingers held up a hand and volunteered to help Melanie appear – to anyone passing by them - to be driving the vehicle. "You sit on me on the seat, and I will take control of your hands and legs," he said, "it'll be just like you're driving it yourself."

With that Melanie slipped into the car, after Something had sat himself down and he then began to take control of her body, a cold breeze coming across her as he began to move her arms and work her legs.

The car was a mess, but it still worked. It appeared that the collision with the tree was not too serious, but people would need to look out for it in the future. The car was just a little dented at the front and wasn't enough for a police car to stop them on a routine check or for an AA or RAC driver to pull up, thinking that a young woman might be in distress.

"Here we go then," she called to all the others in the car, "the Black and Bloody Deathmobile is on the road to Whitchitley Hall – Sébastien Kang, we're coming to hunt you down…"

Chapter 20: 'Sylvia's Mother'

"All Because the Lady Loves..."

Like a James Bond for the fans of dental decay, the people who lounged in front of the television set on a Saturday night, the adverts for Cadbury's Milk Tray were a well anticipated work of action/art. The 'Milk Tray' – identity unknown – would carry out some daring feat, just to arrive in the beautiful woman's apartment and deposit a box of dairy milk chocolates, much to her appreciation when she spots his calling card. Dressed all in black so that he was less easy to spot, he jumped off buildings, exited helicopters, skiing, fighting sharks and more, all in the name of delivering a box of soft centres to someone he fancied! Gary Coombes played the Milk Tray Man from 1968, right through the '70s to 1984.

******

Waiting in the dining room at Whitchitley Hall, Sébastien Kang anticipated contact on the walkie talkie when they (#1 and #7) would get into reception distance and by now, he felt that he should have heard something from them. With a receiving signal at just over two miles, he should have heard some feedback by now, especially as the person in charge was #1 and she could usually be relied on to keep him up to date with operations.

Pacing up and down the polished wooden floorboards, Kang's cane and heels made click clacking noises as he became more and more agitated as the minutes gradually passed and his temper being to flare. Not known for having a caring, kind, or considerate nature, Kang would dish out punishment if the reason for the delay could have been avoided, as any form of holdup was not at all acceptable.

"Excuse me sir, we have a call coming through for you on the walkie talkie," said #6, walking into the dining room on Kang's blindside.

"About time," replied Kang walking towards her and retrieving the receiver off the solid silver tray – Kang had the best equipment, the best cutlery, crockery, furniture, and everything else in between. All the best that money could buy, he bought, and it showed in the opulence of the home that he had made in the wilds of rural Sussex. Kang's lavish lifestyle made him the local celebrity and his team of the M.D.S. were well paid for providing him with the close protective support.

"Hello, it's Kang, what is happening #1 and why the delay?"

The walkie talkie crackled and fizzed as he sent his message and then awaited his reply.

The line then went dead…

Complete silence…

No reply at the other end…

Kang looked at the walkie talkie in his hand and spoke into it again.

"Hello, it's Kang, what is happening #1 and why the delay? Why are you not answering me?"

The receiver crackled and fizzed once more and then went clear, as a message began to be come through.

"Hello Mr. Kang, we need to talk."

Kang looked at the handset in his right hand. He didn't recognise the voice and it certainly was the Eastern European tones of #1 or even #7.

"Who is this?" asked Kang, confused and quizzical as to who was on the line.

"I'm Melanie Moist and I think we need to talk…"

Chapter 21: 'In a Broken Dream'

'A Little Something for the Weekend?'

Incredibly popular during the 1970's with the male population in the UK, Titbits was a weekly publication featuring scandalous stories and articles on film and TV shows. Titbits was well known for featuring glamourous models on the cover, attracting people to the shelf where it was on display. It was described as "Tit-Bits from all the interesting Books, Periodicals, and Newspapers of the World" – so basically it was like a newspaper but covering 'snippets' from everywhere. The magazine wasn't a porn magazine as the name suggested.

******

As the car slowly approached the gates of Whitchitley, Melanie got Something to help her park and turn off the engine, pulling into a layby just outside and then she turned around to address her motley crew.

"Well, here we are," she began, "this is where it will all end, hopefully. I am so, so sorry, at what has happened to all of you and still find it hard to comprehend that you'll all be gone soon. We have been through so much together over the years and this will be the moment that we go through the most terrifying time of our lives."

"And our afterlives," shouted a muffled Minky Bob from the boot of the Cortina.

"Exactly," agreed Melanie, talking to the back of the car.

"Now my suggestion is that I leave the car now and head in after all of you have made your way through the gates and up to the Hall's entrance. They won't be able to see any of you, so it will be a weird entrance for the Cortina, especially when they see the state of it inside. It should frighten the shit out of them and give us the advantage."

All of Melanie's colleagues - that she could see - nodded their heads and then began to filter out of the car. Not having to open any doors, they all just eased themselves through the cars black bodywork and stood as a team around the vehicle, a formidable squad of spirits with an underlying feeling of intense anger and a massive grudge to settle once and for all.

The girls all stood around Melanie and as she gave them a few brief words on what they were going to do, Something started the car and slowly began to turn into the gates and head towards the hall and the inevitable showdown.

Having dragged themselves out of the boot, Minky, Curly, Biffy and Everard walked through the gates and deliberately and determinedly headed up the gravel driveway to the front entrance, following at the rear end of the car - all invisible to the security cameras and all looking extremely serious.

They had one thing on their mind today and that was revenge.

Chapter 22: 'Mouldy Old Dough'

'The Milkybars Are on Me!!!'

Originally beginning in the 1961, the Milkybar Kid was the main advertising campaign for Nestlé Milkybar throughout the 1970's and beyond. With a cast of children, in a western setting, the Milkybar Kid was the towns Sherriff, and he was the one that always saved the day and ended each advert by declaring 'the Milkybars are on me' – there was no end to his generosity, especially with other people's products and at their expense. Henri Nestlé and Daniel Peter invented milk chocolate in 1875 and the first Milkybars were produced in 1936.

******

Inside Whitchitley Hall, in the security office, #6 and #4 watched as the staffs Ford Cortina drove slowly up the drive towards the main doors. All seemed normal at first, until they realised that the vehicle was driverless. They had seen the vehicle being checked out by #1 in the log and she had gone with #7 to collect the '*Moist woman*' from the funeral, so that she could be terminated in person by Kang, but there was no sign of them in the car or the woman they had gone to collect.

The car kept rolling slowly up the driveway, unaided and empty, with no M.D.S. or the stripper from the club in attendance and then, without any reason or notice, the engine kicked in and the car began to race forward, picking up speed as it ploughed forwards towards the entrance to the Hall.

Within the space of 30 seconds, the car made connection with the main doors of the Hall and destroyed them, in a tornado of splinters and flaking paint, as the solid oak doors were pushed inwards, buckling, and coming off their hinges, the remnants of them flying into the hallway and landing on the marble floor. With a hallway and entrance lobby resembling a toothpick factory floor, with small shards and splinters of wood everywhere, the car rolled to a stopped, the front bumper coming to rest on the bottom of the staircase, near where Memory had breathed her last breath on the night of the party, that now seemed so long ago…

#6 and #4 came running from their security watchpoint into the marble entrance way at a pace, their highly polished and cleaned boots sliding across the floor as they came to a stop near the car. As they moved closer to the car all didn't seem right, something was amiss, and it almost seemed like an 'other worldly' event was taking place. The vehicle was completely empty as they had thought from the security cameras, and the doors were all shut, so no one had got out. Moving to the driver's door #6 grabbed the handle and yanked it open and was met with the bloodbath that was now the heavily stained interior of the Ford Cortina Mk III.

Unable to see Something who was sat invisible in the driver's seat #6 leant in and as she did the car's cigarette lighter slowly elevated out of the holder and hovered in the air. Transfixed by this, she just stared as the red-hot lighter flew into her face and made connection with her left eye, gouging in deep and creating a fizzing sound as the red-hot element connected with her eye bulb and burnt it to a frazzled crisp. As she screamed, the lighter moved and did the same actions to her other eye, rendering her totally blind, she letting out an ear-splitting shriek as she rubbed her hands over what was left of her eyes, her eyesight completely gone.

Running to her crew members aid, #4 couldn't see how it had happened, but she was a witness to the aftermath. The remnants of her eyes were charred black remains and she was rubbing vigorously at them with the palms of her hands, as if she was trying to rub sight back into them and repair the lenses, but this was never going to happen, her vision was gone forever, however long forever would be.

Just as the two women stood there, one crying no tears, the other stunned into disbelief, the car moved as if someone was climbing out of it. The suspension lifted as if a weight had been removed from the chassis and then the door swung itself shut with a solid and heavy clunk. As #6 sobbed and mumbled from the pain sinking into her face, #4 could have sworn that she heard footsteps moving from the car towards them, but they were still alone in the ruined hallway – Mr. Kang was not going to be pleased with the mess in his beautiful property and where were the girls and the Moist woman that they had gone to fetch?

Putting her arms around her team-mate as she attempted to take her to the medical facility in their part of the basement, #4 felt a tap on her shoulder and as she turned around, she was hit straight in the face with an alabaster statue of a leopard. The ornament smashed into a thousand pieces as it made a solid connection with her nose, splaying it sideways across her face and causing her to scream in agony - initially due to the shock and then from the searing pain.

Unseen by the two women, Something had climbed out of the car and picked up the figurine from a nearby table in the hall and swung it for all it was worth straight at her, and the distance of the swing gave it the hardest hit imaginable on the bridge of her nose, spraying blood and cartilage across her face and across the still stunned blinded face of #6. Again, not witnessed by the two-security staff, Something walked to the display shelf to the left of the destroyed entrance doors and picked up a large jade lion; typical of the Chinese Fengshui Foo Fu Dog or lion dogs, used to ward off negative energy at entrance hallways to palaces and imperial houses. Something smashed it first down on #4 and then repeated the attack several times on #6, caving in both women's skulls, blood, brains, and fractured bone splitting and spreading across their shoulders as they sunk to their knees, Something repeating the vicious attack several times on both of them; this was vengeance on another scale.

As Something finished the two women off, both breathing their final breaths as he continued to beat their heads to a bloody mashed pulp, the other members of the Golden Palace began to walk in through the door, witnessing the slaughter scene as they entered.

"Oi oi oi, steady on there Something," called Biffo as he led the parade of spirits through the hallway, "I think they won't be causing us anymore problems, step away from the Lion Dog, we have other people to find." And with that, Biffo began to climb the stairs, the other members of his team following him up the staircase, Memory walking the same steps that she came down on her final day.

As they ascended the stairs, the house staff descended them in a hurry to leave the building. Twenty-four staff in total, from maids and cooks to butlers and various other servants, ran down the staircase and out the front door, not wanting to get involved in a gang war, which was what it might have resembled to the innocent passer-by.

Then through the doors strode Melanie Moist, the leader of the pack, the head honcho, the only living member of the Golden Palace entertainment staff and she stood in the hallway, hands on her hips and hollered at the top of her lungs.

"Kang, I'm here..."

Chapter 23: 'Matrimony'

'Everyone's a Fruit & Nut Case...'

Who doesn't remember the catchy tune and the frightfully delightful Frank Muir – him of 'Call My Bluff' on BBC2 – singing the words to the advert whilst inferring that everyone was a little insane for this wonderful chocolate bar. The make-up of chocolate and nuts (almonds) with the addition of raisins (the fruit) were a winning combination and added to the infuriatingly amusing adverts making them extremely popular, as they still are today.

******

S ébastien Kang had heard the car slowly coming up the driveway across the gravel, but had paid little attention to that, until he heard the crash as the car had ploughed through the front doors, demolishing his entrance and causing an unbelievable noise and shaking him out of his thoughts, whilst waiting for the return of the two M.D.S. with the Moist woman.

Kang was in his dining room still, having just drank a cup of lapsang souchong and a eaten a couple digestive biscuits. At the noise he had jumped to his feet and looked out the window to see nothing but a solitary woman in the far distance walking up the drive. Clad all in black, with long dark hair, she looked a little disheveled and like she had been dragged through the literal bush backwards - as the English would say.

As she headed closer, he noticed that she walked with an air of confidence that he rarely saw in women that he dealt with on a personal basis; the M.D.S. were a different female group altogether.

Nearing the front of the house, she looked up at the windows, but due to the tint on them, she was unable to see Kang, but he was able to observe her, and she looked determined.

'This has to be Melanie Moist,' Kang thought to himself as she

went out of view below the window, heading into the house via the front doors. Running quickly back to his bedroom, Kang went to his wardrobe and collected a black box from the base of the closet and opened it up on his bed.

Inside the box was a Luger P08 a German made, Austrian designed, semi-automatic pistol which had been in production since the turn of the century, having been used in Germany up until the 1950's and in many other countries since then. His fingers fumbled with the detachable box magazine as he readied himself to go and face this 'woman'.

He tucked the gun into the rear waistband of his trousers and pulled his polo-necked jumper down over it, just as he heard from downstairs in the entrance hallway –

"Kang, I'm here…"

Chapter 24: 'Run For Home'

''You wouldn't like me when I'm angry...'

Based on the Marvel comic book and produced by the CBS Television Network, 'The Incredible Hulk' was a huge TV series running from 4th November 1977 to 12th May 1982, spanning 80 episodes and 5 TV Movies. Starring Bill Bixby as Dr. David Banner, who after being exposed to gamma radiation turns into his green super-muscled-alter-ego the Incredible Hulk played by Lou Ferrigno. The series covers a reporter who is trying to hunt down the Incredible Hulk, who he thinks killed Dr. Banner and his research partner Dr. Elaina Marks.

Charles Napier who starred in several of the Russ Meyer 'Titsploitation' films in the 1960's and '70s was the voice of the Hulk for season 2-5; for the first two series Ted Cassidy (prior to his death) was the voice of the Hulk, previously known most for being Lurch the butler in the TV series of 'the Addams Family'.

******

In the basement, of Whitchitley Hall, the remaining members of the MDS (#2, #3 and #5) woke up at the sound of the crashing car.

Diving out of their bunks, they bounded towards the staircase to see what the commotion was.

The sight that they were confronted with, was the black Ford Cortina in the foyer of the Hall and the bodies of number #7 and #4, both beaten to death. Their heads were caved in, and pools of blood were already starting to congeal, where a mini lake had already spread across the floor.

They were all completely stunned.

How could this have happened to members of their team? They were trained professionals this sort of thing didn't happen to them.

How could they have been killed so brutally and from what they could see, so easily.

#2 being a bomb expert brought with her three hand grenades and was prepared for using them.

#3 being the expert in handguns, already had her revolver – the Colt .38 Special Cobra - in her shoulder holster and ready for action.

#5 being a marksman with a rifle was currently unarmed as the rifles were all set up at the range downstairs and so she was at a slight disadvantage to the others. She was still ready to kick into action though with her fighting skills, which were also useful.

At that point - just as #5 was considering herself reasonably handy - a noose fell silently from the balcony above, looped perfectly around her neck and with that she was yanked upwards with a force. She was hoisted off the floor as she tried to grab at the rope that was very rapidly strangling her. Dancing like a leather clad puppet on a string, #5 clawed at the rope around her neck, as her eyes began to bulge, and her face gradually turned a hue of blue. Water began to stream down her face as she was yanked up and down on the rope her arms flailing as she tried to grip the rope, which was going nowhere.

#2 and #3 were unable to reach the noose from the hallway and so they both scaled the stairs as fast as they could to confront the person who was pulling on the cord, that was so securely cutting off the life of their colleague. Arriving at the top of the stairs, they stood in horror.

The rope was rigid and was being pulled again and again, by what appeared to be invisible hands – there was no one else on the end of the rope, but it was still held taut by some invisible force.

As they watched the rope and ran forward to try and stop #5 being choked to death, they both failed to notice the two lances from the 'battle display' on the wall, removing themselves and turning to point right at them. If they had been listening carefully then would have heard the noise of the huge spears coming towards them, but all they were involved with at the time was trying to save their team member. The last thing they saw was the rope still tense as the spears rammed right through their backs and then springing out of their chests in a fountain of blood and blades.

Stopped in their tracks, they both looked at each other and then down at the blades protruding from between their breasts. They both gave a random shrug, as neither of them could fathom out what was happening and how it was taking place, with no culprits to be seen.

As the blades were withdrawn, they both collapsed to the floor, on their backs looking upwards, still alive, but on the edge of passing away, in a pool of rapidly expanding blood.

The last thing that #2 and #3 saw was the rope go slack on the banister, followed by a loud crash as #5 hit the floor in the hallway, already deceased and then they saw the sharp and polished blades coming towards their faces.

The lances crashed through their foreheads, both at the same time and then for them it all went black and the final members of the M.D.S. were no more. They were held to the floorboards by the sharp blades, through the front of their heads and wedged deep into the floor of the landing below.

As the light faded for #2 and #3, a voice echoed around the empty hall, empty apart from the bodies strewn across it –

"Kang, I'm here..."

Chapter 25: 'Summerlove Sensation'

'Book 'em Danno...'

Originally released in 1968, the TV series 'Hawaii Five-0' ran right through the 1970's and was massive prime time hit, right up until its end in April 1980. The show followed the exploits of Steve McGarrett played by Jack Lord (who had starred in 'Dr. No' as Felix Leiter) and Danny 'Danno' Williams (played by James MacArthur) who both worked for the Hawaii State Police force, the 'Five-0' referring to the fact that Hawaii at the time was the 50th US state.

The programme ran for 12 seasons with a total of 281 episodes and is still mostly remembered for the amazing theme tune by Morton Stevens.

******

S tanding in the hallway, looking all alone, Melanie Moist tilted her head up and raised her eyes to the stairs and looked for Sébastien Kang.

The scene in the hallway was a scene of carnage and it was all her friends doing.

Though it was all Kang's fault.

He was the cause of the murderous mayhem that had taken place over the last fifteen minutes at his home, and he was the root cause of the deaths of all her friends at the Golden Palace; he had a lot to answer for, both to her and to them.

As she stood there, still drenched in blood from the car journey, she watched as her ghostly acquaintances descended the stairs, not looking pleased with themselves, but looking relieved that most of their work was now complete; only Kang was left.

"Are you ok?" asked Chumpy, as she bounded across the marble floor to stand next to Melanie and survey the butchery on view.

"We made a bit of a mess," said Memory as she crossed the hallway to stand with Melanie as well.

"I think they may all be dead," crooned Nat King Cock, with Minky, Curly, Something, Biffo and Everard nodding in unison.

"What do we do now? Asked Ophelia and with that Katerina, Tuna, Crusty and Fishy all nodded, chipping in with a "yep, what happens next?"

Melanie looked to them all.

All her friends looked up to her and she had to decide what would happen next. Would they go to the police? – might be hard to explain, considering all the dead bodies. Or would they try to find Kang and then wing it from there?

"Ah, Miss Moist, we meet at last," came the voice at the top of the staircase, as Kang appeared and slowly began to walk down the stairs towards her, the seemingly alone and vulnerable 'stripper', stopping halfway.

From where Melanie stood, she was surrounded by thirteen spirit friends. Friends who were so devoted to her that they were helping her from beyond the grave, hopefully aiding their return to a better place in the long run as well.

"You have been quite a thorn in my side, from what I see here. You are a most formidable and unexpected adversary. I never realised that my squad of trained mercenaries would be defeated by one woman on her own. Extraordinary."

Melanie smirked at the speech from Kang. He couldn't see what she could see, and she was hoping that he didn't try to pull anything before she had put an end to his ways.

"I cannot understand how a '*stripper*' on her own, has caused such chaos in my home? How have you destroyed my doors, my car, killed all my bodyguards and still stand there, drenched in blood and not afraid of me in the slightest?"

"It's been a busy day," she smiled and winked at Kang, trying to aggravate him, before she sorted out her problem.

"You have the audacity to come here and do this? We don't have any '*anarchy in the UK*' here, this is beyond my own comprehension."

Melanie just laughed again, chortling behind her hand.

Kang's face began to flush, she was hitting the right points and making him extremely jittery and infuriated. As he began to move further down the stairs, he reached behind his back and pulled out his Luger P08 and pointed it straight at Melanie, as he stepped off the final step on the staircase and stood with his legs splayed and posing like a marksman.

"Any final requests Miss Moist?"

Rubbing her chin, she looked puzzled at Kang, as if she couldn't understand his question. Then out of nowhere she laughed and then said,

"I have come here to settle a score. To end this problem that I've had with you for good and to make sure that nothing like this ever happens at your hands again.

You killed my friends, my work colleagues, my employers. You destroyed what I thought of as a family and you did it for greed. You took everything that was dear to me and got rid of it forever. I attended the funeral today of twelve of my friends and the thirteenth one was murdered here – in your hallway – on the night of your party, all because you wanted to destroy our club and build some more of your properties.

Empire building pure and simple and at the expense and lives of genuine people. Genuine working-class people who had families, wives, children – you ended it all for them, there's only me left and it's just not fair what you've done and now it will have to end."

Kang looked at her aghast at her comments and the disrespect that she felt towards him.

A member of the Chinese old school. Hong Kong aristocracy, how dare she speak to him this way, there was no way that she could talk to him like this, and she'd cracked and shattered his priceless Chinese Fengshui Foo Fu Dog's as well, which must be a bad omen for her.

"I'm sorry you feel like this, but now it's goodbye, my problem with you is over." With that as Kang aimed to shoot at Melanie, his Luger was wrestled out of his hand by an unseen force and he was pistol whipped across the face, stunning him, and making him stumble back a couple steps to the bottom of the staircase once more.

"How did you do that?" Kang asked, completely confused as to what had just happened. Then immediately he felt hands pushing him down onto the stairs, not visible hands, but cold and clammy invisible ones and then they held him there, as the temperature began to drop in the hallway and the atmosphere took a turn for the worse.

As he lay there pinned to the stairs by the ghostly entities, he squinted and when he did, he could see that he was not alone. There were more than a dozen people there - working-class-people - touching him inappropriately as he was splayed out across his expensive marble staircase.

"Any final requests?" she asked.

"Yes, who are you?" demanded Kang, looking terrified and confused all at the same time.

"I'm Miss Melanie Moist, the sole survivor of the Golden Palace stripper troupe and now it's goodbye from me."

As the final words passed from her lips, she left the hallway and walked into the ballroom, just as Memory pulled the pins and stuffed two of the hand grenades - that #2 had been carrying - down the front of his trousers.

"Aaaaaagggggghhhhh!!!!" screamed Kang as he realised his fate and seconds later, he exploded in a ball of blood, bone, tissue, and hatred.

******

Minutes later when the dust had finally settled, Melanie strode back into the hallway and the scene was worse than it was before.

"I've just gone and blown his bloody balls off," said Memory smiling, feeling that she finally had some form of closure.

Melanie looked at the mess. She may have removed Kang's testicles, but in the process had also ruined his rib cage, shattered his hips, crushed his calves, and spread his intestines out across the staircase like bunting; a garland of gory guts, dripping blood onto the stairs and adding to the other dead bodies and body parts, that were already there. The previously beautiful white walls had been sprayed crimson, with chunks of Kang stuck to its surface like fleshy warts.

"Well, I think that's the end of Kang," said Melanie as she surveyed the scene, making it difficult not to urge, the amount of death on show was turning her stomach.

"I think you could be right," agreed Biffo as he stood beside Melanie with everyone else, surveying the remains of the man who had organised their demise as a group.

"Well as we are here alone now, I think that we should have a quick look around," began Melanie, looking at her friends for agreement.

All her ghostly compadres agreed, and they followed her up the blood-soaked staircase, Melanie tip toeing through the remains of Kang, pushing his head away with her foot as she carried on to the top of the stairs.

Wandering around the house for the next hour, they went as a team, from room to room to room. They checked out all the upstairs guest bedrooms and the study plus the bathrooms. Eventually they came to the bedroom that had belonged to Kang.

With satin sheets and the finest Egyptian cotton pillowcases and a heavy cotton throw, his bedroom was obviously the most luxurious of all the sleeping quarters in the house and it showed, but what she hoped was there, was hidden in the large triple wardrobe.

Melanie flung open the wardrobe doors and what she expected to be in there, was there in the bottom of the unit on the floor, Kang's safe. "I thought this would have been where he'd have it hidden," she cooed, feeling extremely pleased with herself. "If only we could open it up and find out how much he's stored in there, before any of his cronies come here looking for it."

"Let me have a check for you," said Everard, as he bent down in front of the 15" by 15" by 15" solid cast iron safe. Leaning in towards the safe, his head went through the front, and he looked around in there for a few moments alone.

"You won't believe what's in there," smiled Everard, looking like the cat who'd got not only the cream, but half the cow to go with it and a milk maid on top, when he finally pulled his head back out.

"Spill."

"It's full of money. Bundles and bundles of ten-pound notes. There must be at least £150,000 in there, possibly a lot more, you are one very lucky lady."

Melanie looked around at them all and said –

"I'm not lucky, I've lost all of you, my friends."

All the spirits and Melanie tried to stifle a sob, suppressing how upset they all actually were. They really would miss each other, and it would be difficult to carry on without them, for Melanie on her own.

"It doesn't have to be like this," began Biffo, "we could always stay around with you, we don't have to leave limbo if we don't want to, do we?"

Everyone nodded their heads and agreed.

"That's a deal then, we ain't going anywhere. We'll stay and help you and let's build another club, bigger and better than the last one," said Biffo and everyone nodded in complete agreement.

"I'd have missed you too much anyway," said Chumpy and the other girls all nodded.

"OK then. So, what we need to do is somehow move this safe downstairs and put it in a vehicle and drive the hell out of here, before the police or Kang's colleagues turn up," hollered Melanie, rounding up the troupes and making a plan.

With that the spirits – all acting as one – in full on poltergeist mode, lifted the safe and walked it down the stairs to the basement of Whitchitley Hall and deposited it in the back of a large Ford Supervan. Ophelia went up to the security office and retrieved the set of keys and with Something driving and Melanie looking like she was driving, they prepared to leave the Hall and head back to central London.

"I know someone who can safe crack the safe for us, we'll go and see him, and you tell him that I was the one who told you about him, it'll be fine," said Biffo as they left the basement and headed out into the grounds.

Just as they began to leave, they spotted someone wandering around by the maze area and like them, she was slightly see-through and floating above the ground, moving about like a lost soul.

"I'll go have a word," said Chumpy, leaving the van and moving across the grounds to where the apparition was pacing and looking bewildered.

As they watched, Chumpy returned to the van, with the woman all in leather following them.

"This is #8, she was killed at the orders of Kang's #1, she's a lost soul just like us – can she join us?"

"Of course," said Melanie, bidding her welcome into the back of the van, which was already crowded with the 'Unlucky Thirteen', "the more people we have to help, the better our combined results will be. Welcome aboard #8, do you wanna be in my gang?"

Melanie smiled and with that, the van drove off, heading back to London and new times ahead.

The Soundtrack to 'Get Moist'

'Gudbuy T'Jane' - Slade

Released in 1972 and hitting #2 on the Top 40, another hit from the UK chart legends, gaining another silver disk.

'Alligator Man' - Stoneground

Formed in Concord, California, this single was featured in the party scene in the Hammer film 'Dracula A.D. 1972'.

'Young Hearts Run Free' - Candi Staton

A disco mega-hit from 1976, hit #1 in the US and #2 in the UK by the Christian singer from Alabama.

'Sugar Baby Love' - The Rubettes

Was labelled a 'bubblegum pop' song from 1974 and was the bands only #1 in the UK

'Thank You For Being Friend' - Andrew Gold

Released in 1978, this single was covered by Cynthia Fee for 'the Golden Girls' TV Show.

'Move On Up' - Curtis Mayfield

A soul classic released in the UK in 1971, reaching #12. The album version is nearly 9 minutes in length.

'Shout It Out Loud' - KISS

From the classic KISS album 'Destroyer', this was a #1 single in Canada and was the second single to hit the Top 40 in the US - but failed to chart in the UK in 1976.

'It Never Rains in Southern California' – Albert Hammond

A #2 single in the US in 1972 and most surprisingly a #1 in Japan. Albert is the father of the Strokes guitarist Albert Hammond Jr.

'*Make It With You*' - *Bread*

The band's first Top Ten hit in the US in 1970 reaching #1, it also hit #5 in the UK.

'*Lido Shuffle*' - *Boz Scaggs*

A hit in 1977 reaching #11 in the US, #13 in the UK and the biggest hit in Australia where it spent 3 weeks at #2.

'*Rhinestone Cowboy*' - *Glen Campbell*

A huge country in and a classic of the genre in 1975. A #1 chart success in the US, Canada, and Ireland. A #4 in the UK as well. Was a hit with both the Pop and Country fans.

'*Kid Charlemagne*' - *Steely Dan*

A very low charting single in 1976, only making it to #82 in the US, it's still a well-loved classic of the era.

'Hold the Line' - Toto

The first single from the first Toto album, a #5 hit in the US and hitting #14 in the UK in 1978.

'If You Leave me Now' - Chicago

A #1 single in the US in 1976 and in the UK, South Africa, Ireland, Netherlands, Canada, and Australia too.

'Vincent' - Don McLean

Based around the life of the artist Vincent van Gogh, this song is based partly on the painting 'The Starry Night' by van Gogh. The single was a #1 in the UK, Ireland, Italy and a #2 on the Easy Listening chart in the US in 1972.

'Drift Away' - Dobie Gray

A big hit in 1973, this cover version of the Mentor Williams song became a hit for Dobie Gray, reaching #5 and #7 in Canada.

'Big Yellow Taxi' - Joni Mitchell

Was a hit in 1970 at #11 in the UK, #14 in Canada, #6 in Australia, but only reaching #67 in the US – a different version was released in the US in 1974 and then reached #24.

'Babe' – Styx

The bands only UK hit at #6, #1 in the US, #1 in South Africa and #1 in Canada. It was the last char topper of the 1970's and the first of the 1980's in many countries.

'Barracuda' - Heart

A #11 hit in the US in 1977 and still a popular song by the Wilson sisters, Ann and Nancy, the lead single from the early Heart album 'Little Queen'.

'Refugee' - Tom Petty & the Heartbreakers

The song was recorded by Tom and his band and included on the album 'Damn the Torpedoes' but, was not released as a single until January 1980. It reached #15 in the US

'Sylvia's Mother' –

Dr. Hook & the Medicine Show

The first hit for the band in 1971, reaching #2 in the UK, #5 in the US and a #1 in South Africa, Ireland, Australia and New Zealand.

'In a Broken Dream' - Python Lee Jackson

Released in 1972 and hit #3 in the UK, even though Rod Stewart's name was not mentioned on the single or the cover but was known to be the singer on the song – which is obvious.

'Mouldy Old Dough' - Lieutenant Pigeon

A one hit wonder hit for the band in 1972, but a #1 in the UK, New Zealand, Belgium, and Ireland.

'Matrimony' - Gilbert O'Sullivan

A song from the 1971 album 'Himself' and more of a single than any other track on the album.

'Run For Home' - Lindisfarne

The first single from the 1978 album 'Back and Fourth', reaching #22 on the UK charts

'Summerlove Sensation' - Bay City Rollers

Another hit for one of the first UK 'Boy Bands', reaching #3 on the UK chart in 1974 for the tartan clad army of fans to adore.

Other Books by Ian Carroll

The History of Rock Music at Donington Park – Covering all the bands with hundreds of exclusive interviews.

The Book of the Lock-Down in Plymouth in 2020 – through the eyes of the Plymouth Population and photos.

The Official Book of the Reading Festival Volume One – From the beginning of the Festival up to 2006 – Second Volume in process now.

The Guide to all the Amityville Horror Movies over the last five decades.

Monsters of Rock – One half of the above Book – see also the Download Festival Book as well.

The Book of the Cornwall Coliseum in St. Austell – the greatest southwest venue of all time.

The Guide to all the Hammer Horror films, from the 1950's to the 1970's.

Scary Short Stories to dip into on a cold winter's night or on your holidays.

A terrifying tale, told in a blood thirsty extreme way with co-author Paddy Mullen.

The Reel Cinema in Plymouth campaign to save it.

Terrifying tale of a clown terrorising the occupants of a supermarket and following up his killing spree at a fancy-dress party.

A guide to the Netflix Horror movie sensation from 2021 – filled with photos, posters and opinions.

Photo Guide to the Reel/Canon/MGM/ABC cinema in Plymouth which closed in 2019.

The Unofficial Guide to the Movie – 'Henry Portrait of a Serial Killer'. Featuring lots of photos and posters.

A murderous tale of Mermaids, set on a small island with a lighthouse, with a boats crew who've been stuck there.

Internet Dating can be a dangerous hobby and the people in this book find that out at first hand.

Printed in Great Britain
by Amazon